Blossom to Bone

A collection of original poetry

Lorelei Greenwood-Jones

ISBN: 9798737438081

Independently published

DEDICATION

Travis, Carter, and all my Beloved Ones who have inspired me in this last year – my sincere thanks and blessings.

And to the Goddess Brighid, my nightly muse.

CONTENTS

Lorelei Greenwood-Jones

A few words of introduction

In December of 2020, I set myself a challenge of writing every night for 100 days. I used to write a lot but fell out of the habit in the last few years. It was a wonderful exercise – even when I was tired and thought no inspiration would come, something always appeared.

Not every piece from the 100 made it to this book, but most of them did. I shared each poem (friends only) to my Facebook page and sometimes to Fire in the Head (a poetry page dedicated to the saint/goddess Brighid).

In recent years, I have delighted in discovering books of modern faerie tales and fantasy, many of them edited by Ellen Datlow and Terri Windling. Charles de Lint has also been a favorite. These books have led me toward writing poetry and stories in a way that is new to me but that intrigue my creative side.

In this book, you'll find beauty, fear, enchantment, strange twists, wonder, and things that may give you food for thought.

Happy reading!

Lorelei Greenwood-Jones

Prayer Wheel

The prayer wheels turn,
every spin a blessing,
a revolution of kindness,
each cycle brings hope.
Sacred words move
in a dizzying dance
and my feet follow.
Smoothly gliding,
graceful as swan,
strong as oak,
flexible as stems of grain
bending before the wind.
Floating like feathers
my hands flutter,
birds impossible to capture,
singing songs
in silence.
Temple bells chime,
each note a glistening drop
of water in a holy pool.
I am filled
and emptied
and filled in turn.
I have no fear of emptiness.
I have no need
to fill the spaces
with more than I can afford.
I have no need
of noise to fill my ears,
for magick lives
in the silence
between the notes.
Nor have I desire
for sweets to fill my mouth -
indeed, praise to my Gods
will be sweeter
and will end my hunger.
Thirst shall be slaked
with cherished libation
as I pour a portion
on the sacred ground,
the soil of my Mother
the earth.
From Her body do we come,

one day to return,
then once again rise
to live once more,
and I shall sing
of my love for Her
with every breath
of every life I am given.

Fire

Fire burns in the hearth,
a hungry being
fed by the death of trees.
Sparks fly
as the resin pops,
the lifeblood
of those trees
stilled
but flying upward now
in a deathdance,
the last glow
of life.
Transformation,
the gift of change
as the flames
devour their food,
altering shape and form,
altering substance,
until naught is left
but ashes
and a lingering scent
of wood smoke.

Lorelei Greenwood-Jones

Weight

What weight
is on my shoulders?
What burdens
do I still bear
that others have forgotten
in the endless run of time?
I find myself
pondering worthiness
of my own self.
With highs and lows
even as the tide rolls on
and the Moon
moves in her phases,
so do our own lives move.
Balance is fleeting,
joy but a taste.
We cannot, I cannot,
wallow in degradation,
in regret
once atonement is cast
and the lesson learned.
And yet my thoughts
fall back onto the road
long traveled,
never gently
but time and again.
Moths and flames.
I burn within.
But, too,
from where shall peace come
if not from within?
For the sake of my heart,
love shall come;
with a shift in my soul,
forgiveness.
Someday.

A Decision

And from there on, she ceased caring about the less important things in her life. They were taking up space, setting her thoughts whirling at unquiet speeds. She was so done with the frantic voices in her head, the nonsensical dialogues that pervaded her thinking, especially when her hands were engaged in other tasks. It was her job to be a decent human, not to kowtow to the whims and imagined opinions of others. That meant also being kind to herself, perhaps most of all. The things she said to herself she could not imagine saying to a loved one – the very thought horrified her. But is she not herself a loved one? Didn't she deserve the respect she showed others? It was hard for her to look into her own eyes in the mirror and choose to believe she is worthy.

But she is.

Faerie

Bejeweled
her gossamer wings
glitter with dew
from the newborn day.
The scent of flowers
and fresh breezes
lifts her spirits
and her delicate form
rose above the grasses.
If you listen
very closely
you can hear
with each flutter
a sound of tiny bells
chiming
in the early sunlight.

Ink

Pain with a purpose
this ink that she plies
wrought from a drawing
within my mind's eyes.
The thought becomes action,
ideas turned real -
machinery buzzes
and ink flows through steel.
One line, then another
and color comes through
laid in my skin
til the pattern's in view -
design of my spirit
and song of my heart -
this pain with a purpose,
this pain becomes art.
Forever displayed
on my body, my skin,
this meaningful method
to share what's within.
It tells of my story
and speaks my life's tale -
accepting the needles
I open the veil.
The drumming, it brings me
such peace in this place,
a living room turned
into such sacred space.
I sing along boldly,
my heart does the same -
so holy, this marking,
this purposeful pain.

Sharing the Love

Lend to me your hand
your heart
the compassion that lights you from within
for I am of you and you of me,
we, sisters and brothers all.
Bring to me your breath
your voice
that we may sing together
of the wonders of this world
for many are Nature's gifts
and there is beauty for the eye that will see.
Give to me your passion
your fire
that energizes thoughts and brings them to action
a fruiting of ideas
to lead us to progress,
tho not for the sake of progress alone.
Paint for me the things you love
the things that bring you joy
and share them far and wide
that all can bear witness to the outpouring
of your spirit.
Set for me a spot at your table
at your welcome place
that I may be nourished and nourish others in turn
for all deserve to be fed
and all deserve inclusion.
Bring to me your pain
your woundedness
your broken heart and shattered dreams
that I may mend as I am able
and soothe where mending cannot hold.
Speak to me of your aspirations
of plans and seeds planted in rich soil
and we shall water them together
with the sweet libation of clear springs
flowing from between the stones
with its source deep in the earth
and as those seeds bear fruit
we shall together share the fortune
with all who lack
and bring the world to comfort.

Love

On the altar of my heart
lies a full cup
brimming with delight of our love
and still with the peace of constancy.
There too abides the joy
of our shared laughter
the wonder of our adventures
the companionship
from which I need little rest.
Home is where you are.

Pixie Led

(for Vince)

On, around, beyond, and under,
Off I wander, here and there.
Left to go by bluster, blunder,
I am lost, but oh, but where?
Prick of holly, sting of nettle,
Tangled ivy in my hair -
Stop do I and try to settle
But I dasn't rest, nor dare.
Creeping softly through the leaf mould
Tiny feet and knees parade -
Some are shy and some be quite bold
this light-wing-ed cavalcade.
Blossoms glow and twigs be shaken,
rings 'round my astonished form.
Where they go I shall be taken
Quick diverging from the norm.
Fires flit and sparkles linger
wisps of fog and shining eyes.
Whirling dance, they take my finger,
I can do naught with surprise.
On they guide me through the treelands
Nothing I can do but go.
Wishing long to see my freelands -
just this Pixie realm I know.
Merry dance and honeyed liquor
fed to me in acorn caps.
Beg to leave, they only snicker -

I be caught within their traps.
Moon goes down and starshine fading,
golden sun peeks 'bove the hill.
Pixies end their serenading
Leaving me alone and still.
Stumble-step and knock-kneed wander
back to my beloved realm,
pause do I to think and ponder,
but my senses overwhelm.
Shall I ever on remember?
Am I able to recall
with this quickly dying ember
those whose spell I did befall?

Brighid

This day, this morning,
I welcomed you in
O Brighid the lady of fire.
I made for you cakes
and shortbread so thin
O Brighid, the lady of all.
Milk dressed with honey
I laid out for you
O Brighid, the lady of wells.
With water so sweet
by spring or by dew
O Brighid, the lady of all.
Stood at the threshold
and called out your name
O Brighid, the lady of healing.
The Brat I left out
surely told me you came
O Brighid, the lady of all.
With song on my lips
I rang the fair bells
O Brighid, the lady of arts.
And wrote you a poem
that made my heart swell
O Brighid, the lady of all.

Enchanted Wood

"I love her hair," he said
as he watched the waves
cascade down the stones
of the tower
once more.
Golden like honey
her locks dripped with sunshine
warm and inviting
to the young swain below.
Ascending swiftly
he gathered her into his arms
and spoke to her
words of adoration
that fell upon her ears
like kisses.
Far less shy than before
she answered his caresses
with those of her own
her hands dancing along his smooth muscles
his dark hands in her hair.
In his deep brown eyes
was the question
and she answered with her own
acquiescing silently.
They fell among the silks
her hair and the soft bedding
like rabbits amidst clover
as they nibbled away
each others' innocence
with joy and increasing fervor.
When at last they lay spent
basking in the glow of shared peaks
their talk turned to freedom
and commitment.
He promised to return
with his brothers
and ropes to secure her release
for she could not descend on her own tresses.
The young man had been drawn to the tower
from his ramble in the woods
by the sound of her singing
and weeping
and wondered who could keep such beauty
locked away from all other eyes.

The old woman
had passed some time before
leaving no provision
to set the girl free
and with her died her reasoning
of this strange entrapment.
He took his leave
with words of love.
Early the next morning
he appeared with three
fine young men,
his brothers surely.
He ascended her sunny length
as did one other with him
to make fast the rope
to lower her from this stony height
to a far better life below.
Carefully was she drawn down
her first time, they presumed,
out of the keep.
Her feet touched earth
soiling her perfect slippers
that had never seen dirt.
As the four brothers led her
into the woods and away from the tower
her flowing hair gathered twigs
moss
sticks
caught on branches
swept the long grasses.
Distressed, she gathered
her golden waves about her
adding the detritus
to her fine gown.
She began to limp
her thin shoes no match
for the rocks and roots
in her path.
A jagged note
came to mar her melodic voice
rendering sharp tones
as she complained
about her discomfort.
But the men seemed not to hear
appeared not to see.
The way seemed very long
and without end
and she was growing weary

unused to such activities
that taxed her far more
than embroidery or music.
Grown impatient with their disinterest
she halted in her tracks
but the young men saw not
continued walking
silently moving further down
the wooded path.
She called out to them
a screech of anger
no more song in her speech.
They did not hear.
Soon they were out of view
and the girl stood
stunned
wondering at her plight.
She knew not the ways of the forest
nor of any of the world
outside of her rooms
in the now-distant tower
did not know how to get back
and could not have ascended
had she wished to.
Strange noises surrounded her
creatures unseen
crunched the fallen leaves
causing her to look about
in consternation.
Her thirst made demands
that she could not answer
and her stomach was empty.
Defeated, she sat heavily
under a tall oak tree
(she did not know it was named thus)
and leaned back
against the firm trunk.
No tears left her eyes
to make trails in the dust
that decorated her face.
Neither did she cry aloud
but kept her anguish
in her heart.
She remained there
motionless
as the day passed
and the chill of evening
set about her.

The light between the trees
already thin and dull
turned gray
and night came on.
She made no sound
moved not at all.
Slight rustling sounds came
a shifting, slithering
and the roots of the oak
began to move of their own accord
binding first her ankles
then legs
hands
torso
slowly
though she was not aware.
The grooves of the bark
widened
drew her in
capturing her very essence
as the stone tower never had.
By the time a dim dawn came
there was naught left
but a tattered silk slipper
soiled and torn
the remaining beads
winking in the low light.

Lorelei Greenwood-Jones

Spring

Come 'round to full moon once more,
Her Ladyship riding high
in the eastern sky
illumined and lustrous,
writing silver sigils on snow
with moonlight and tree branches,
shadow words
only understood by mages
in ages gone by.

Come through the four weeks passing,
of time and tide flowing
waning and growing,
she's danced in our dreams
and brought us the visions
that haunt and inspire,
turning thought into action,
images and passion to fruition,
trusting intuition to our glory.

Come into new seasons, to blossoms
from the waking earth
a slow rebirth,
growth on her own terms,
first small and vague, weak,
but gaining in vigor, building,
changes accepted as inevitable,
sampling sunlight,
delighting in its warmth.

Come by the gardens in spring,
new birds singing,
bees fly near, winging
to dance the maps of pollen
and nectar to sip,
to bring home the golden treasure
for the life-giving sweetness
made in waxen shells
and cells containing new life.

March

The wild winds of March
have come to my door -
they howl in the treetops
and blow 'cross my floor.
They come in the crevices,
enter the cracks -
springtime will come
and there's no going back.

The gales speak with voices -
so loudly they shout
to be let indoors
or for me to come out.
They rattle the branches,
they lift the dead leaves.
"Remember dead winter!"
they call on the breeze.

But Winter's hold's broken
tho He may still fuss
and hurl, with invective,
more storms right at us.
We'll weather them calmly
and wait for the days
when sunshine takes over
from Winter's cold ways.

So as the days lengthen
the calendar turns
to far fairer hours,
to flowers and ferns
and March, like a lion,
has come with a roar,
come singing of springtime
for us to adore.

Blessingway

There is a being
of starlight and wonder
inside of your body,
the two of you
joined in the most intimate of bonds
that can ever be.
Though you've yet never seen one another,
there is love.
You are Mother;
you are Goddess.
Always will you recall
the feeling of that first kick,
the earliest stirrings of life
in your very center.
Your mother
and her mothers before her
and all their mothers
back into the mists of time
culminate within you,
an unbroken lineage of love.
Resting beneath your heart
is the most perfect creation,
a most delicate creature,
waiting contentedly.
What joy and amazement,
what delight in this miracle.
These weeks will pass,
both taking forever
and moving in a flash.
Enjoy each precious moment -
the bubbles and wiggles,
the tiny foot under your ribs
(no slouching for you),
playing Guess-The-Body-Part
as your child shifts
within your womb.
And when it is your time at last,
may the Way open easily for you,
as your body knows
just what to do.
And when you see your child
for the first time,
you shall know true love.

Otro

Otro woke in confusion. It was mostly dark but for a brief flicker of flame in the distance, and it was cool, somewhat damp. Stretching their neck, they looked about as best they could. Upon moving their arm, they discovered a long silver chain binding them to a ring in the stone floor. Worry began to turn to panic – just where were they and why? The chain was solid, allowing them a small circle in which to move. Exploring the circumference of the chain's reach, they bumped into a small table which, they found, contained a candlestick, some lucifers, and a large container of water. They lit the candle and looked suspiciously at the water. Then taking up the light, Otro finished their travel around the restricted area – stone floor, stone (they presumed) walls just outside of vision, and... what was that? A glint. A shine. Reaching far forward with the candle, they squinted, gasped. Why, that was gold! Gems! Silver! Bejeweled chalices and pieces of shiny armor, mirrors and coins of strange pressing. What treasure they had come upon!

But just past the wonderment came a chilling realization followed by a snort of derision. Surely the stories could not be true. These things were myths, weren't they? Had to be. Creatures like... well, like the ones in the tales told around the fire. Complete bish-bosh. Otro snorted again.

And so did something down the tunnel.

They drew a fast breath, held it, closed their eyes. No no no no no no......

Something breathed on them, a warm whoosh flaring their hair about their head.

"But yes."

If stones could speak, they would sound like this voice. Not so much gravelly as earthy, like large rocks grinding slowly past one another. Otro swallowed, kept their eyes firmly shut.

"I wonder, which will win out first, your curiosity or your fear?" the voice rumbled.

Otro wondered, too.

"My... my family has no money," they stammered. "You won't get any treasure for me."

The beast sighed. "Stories precede me, I imagine. Oh all they want is gold and jewels and a tasty virgin to munch. Blech! I know what you young people eat these days, and let me tell you, it does nothing for your flavor. A nice fat sheep, though, that hits the spot."

Otro opened one eye. "You're not going to eat me then?"

A set of wicked teeth flashed into a grin before them, and they nearly wet themself.

"Do you want to be eaten?"

"No! No definitely not not me no way I'm skinny I'm gamey look at me I'd go right to your hips..."

A bellow of laughter stopped them in mid-sentence. Otro opened their other eye.

Before them lay a creature of such grand proportions as to make all the fireside stories a pale mimicry. Green scales, pointed ears, silver tipped claws, a tail longer than a large canoe. Yes. It was a dragon.

Otro thought about their likely plight. No one from the village would bother looking for them for days; they often set out alone with a book or two, wandering off to a favorite nook by a burbling stream or a half dozen other quiet spots. And even if someone cared enough to look, would they ever find this cavern? The hillsides were riddled with similar holes, most of them unexplored.

Since ingestion was off the menu, if the beast could be believed, then what might this creature want from them? Surely there was enough treasure by far to purchase anything it wanted. Able to wait no more, Otro inquired.

"Want?" repeated the dragon. "Why, something only someone like you could provide. I shall return shortly." It wandered out of the small circle of candle light and shuffled down a corridor. There was a series of muffled thumps, a small curse, and then a sliding scraping sort of noise. Otro's heart fluttered again.

As the beast came back into view, Otro could see that it held something in its teeth. A leather strap, quite hefty and wide, and behind that...

"Books!" they exclaimed, between curiosity and joy.

"Yeth," lisped the dragon, strap still in its teeth. "I want you to read to me."

"But surely someone of your intelligence and age could read..." they began.

The dragon spat out the leather and pointed a rapier claw at them. "Don't impugn my intelligence, young human. Brains I have in plenty. It's the dexterity I lack." It turned up its paw, showing all the talons. "Do you think I can turn a delicate page with these? That I can chuckle at an amusing passage without chancing the paper getting singed? Long have I tried and all have I failed. I am desperate to be removed from this place and sent to inspiring lands of another's imagination. I want to be carried away from myself. I want," the dragon said seriously, "you to read to me."

Otro's hopes buoyed, then flagged.

"Am I to be your slave then?" they asked. "Am I to be chained here for all time?"

"Oh that? Nah, that was just to keep you from wandering into the caverns and getting lost or hurt. There are some mighty dropoffs around here." And with that, the dragon snicked out a claw and pulled the link closest to Otro's wrist cuff. The chain slithered to the cave floor with a musical sound. Otro took a closer look at the cuff that remained – such beautiful etching! What a grand piece!

"Now," grunted the dragon, settling itself to the ground, "look through that stack of books and choose one to begin with."

They looked at the stack. Hmmm, not an awful lot there. It would be no time at all before they finished the books... and then what? Back to the village where they were mainly misunderstood, where there was no real opportunity for growth or escape?

As if reading their expression, the dragon cracked another toothy grin. "Fear not, youngling – there are hundreds of books in the salt cave. Keeps 'em dry in there."

Hundreds... Otro looked again at the books. Several of them were very old with intriguing covers and, as they flipped through, fantastic drawings. They nearly began to salivate. There were only so many books in the village, and they had read all of them at least once, returning to a favorite here and a well-loved tome there.

Hundreds...

After a bit of hunting for a comfortable cushion and a few more candles, Otro and the dragon settled in. Eyes gleaming, they opened the first book.

Limbo

The list of what to do
grows ever longer
feels unmotivating
in this dim late winter.
Filling the time
aimlessly searching
not sad exactly
but directionless
listless
wanting but not able.
This is the conundrum.
The juice
has been sucked out
leaving me
with a husk
that does not nourish
and the memory
of that delicious moment
catches between pain
and sweetness.
Limbo.
Set in the center
of life and immobility
I wait for spring.

Lorelei Greenwood-Jones

Between

Betwixt and between
unknown and unseen
the Seelie court
ride over the green

on foot and on horse
past heather and gorse
they flow with the light
as a matter of course

some dressed in white
and more, colors bright
singing a song
of immortal delight

and part of the throng
where they know they belong
keep time with their drum
that moves them along.

You feel worrisome
that you may just succumb
to the merriment played
by the group frolicsome.

And in you shall wade
all your plans be waylaid
by the tune in your head
and the grand serenade

and walk ye instead
with the very high-bred
decisions forgo
protestations unsaid.

The years you'll not know
and no older you'll grow
where none intervene
in this realm deep below.

Nitenite

Peaceful evening ends
The hour grows late, my dear one
Time to go to sleep

No more TV now
Five minutes more? No way, dude
Get your butt undressed

Protesting loudly
Jammies do not go on well
Flailing arms and legs

Now go brush your teeth
No, really, use your toothpaste
Ew! Go brush again

OK, one last drink
I won't go to the kitchen
Bathroom water's fine

Favorite story read
Pillow fluffed and covers on
Close those sleepy eyes

Here is your stuffie
And that one, and this one too
Where's the kid in here?

Under bed is checked
Not a monster in sight, dear
Really, go to sleep

Not sleepy, nuh-uh
Never been more awake, mom
I'm not sleepy zzzzzz

Now I'M all worn out
Maybe one more TV show
Couch is so soft zzzzzz

Lorelei Greenwood-Jones

Vision

In the vision that I was graced
I came to a temple
and within it, a spring
welling up with sweetest water
clear and healing
and I knew it to be of Brighid.
The columns were marble
placed in a broad circle
encircling the spring,
and the spring itself
bordered by stones.
Women gathered
from every race and time
to touch the sacred essence
and be freed
cleansed
of all fear and derision
of our women's blood.
All the stories
of shame and blame
fell from our bodies like scales
leaving us fresh and whole.
We were lifted
buoyed
held aloft as the holy beings that we are,
able, some for the first time,
to walk in our own skin
without feeling the pressing
of opinions of our worth.
We joined in a cave
just beyond the temple
and bled upon the earth,
a gift for a gift.
As one whose blood has ceased to flow,
I thought back to those days,
feeling sad that I did not know
to lay my blood upon the land.
But sorrow did not linger
for in the presence
of this divine womanhood,
a golden light emanated from my womb
and flowed down through the earth
to the womb of the Mother.
I felt I was meeting my own self.
And high above

in the blackness of the night sky
the Moon sang my song,
knowing fully
that she is connected
to the blood that once flowed
from that holy vessel within me.
And I,
between the Earth and the Moon,
between Mother and Sister,
I breathed my gratitude
as a prayer
and found myself within.

Quarantine Cooking

The scent
of an Unidentified Frying Object
came hurtling through the air
like a baton
whirling
caught by your nose
and doing similar damage.
Dear gods
what did he burn now?
It smelled like sneakers
with a side of bacon
and laces
like a pallid garnish
set weakly down
beside a pool of...
well, just of.
Culinary masters of the world,
hide in fear
for your nemesis
has arisen
from the depths of the internet
with a burning
(and I mean that)
desire to cook.
For someone
who thought of a frypan
as a weapon
he is surely discovering new uses
for cookery

in his arsenal.
Not being able
to eat out for a year
has seriously marred his psyche
causing him
to reach out to the web
and seek out foodie delights
that become, in his hands,
ordinance.
Applause for effort
but a hero's parade
for disposing of that... that.
And I, in the meantime,
desperately look up a copy
of Cooking For Dummies
for next-day delivery.

Writing

"Set pen to paper," said he
"and release the vision inside you."
She was hesitant.
Would it be worthy?
Could she find the eloquence
that she heard in her head
and translate it
to the written word?
She knew to find words
that struck the ear
with a blossom rather than a brick
(tho indeed, at times
bricks were appropriate).
To free her imagination
was a gift
she had not before known -
it was as much frightening
as liberating.
Tumbling through such sophomoric prose
as in her early years
(she was embarrassed to read
her young works)
made her hesitant
to express emotion
dream

depth of heart.
"In our newness," he said
"we all inscribe drivel and dross
but reach through your experience
and bring forth the gold."
But where to begin, she wondered.
Where lies the spark
that ignites the inner flame?
She looked about her room
seeing the same items
that were present every day -
nothing exciting there.
But...
perhaps...
In her collection of objects
from her travels
there were memories
sparkling at the edge of inspiration
whispering "Tell my story."
She had gotten so used
to seeing all around her
the familiar items
of her day-to-day -
hadn't they once held magic?
Weren't they given place
in her living space
as a solid reminder
of the paths she had traversed?
Oh yes
there was gold there.
And setting pen to paper
she began.

Grace

Make of my body an altar
a sacred vessel that holds within it
a heart that overflows with love
giving from the desire to give
endless in its capacity to cherish
a wellspring of empathy and caring.

Let my ears hear
what is truly being spoken
and what is left unsaid
that I may determine
how best to aid another.

Bring me eyes that can see
both in darkness and in light
that can see the gradients and values
of all the grays in between.

Open my hands
that I may reach out to others
to lift them up
raise them up
hold those who are in need of comfort
and accept comfort in return.

Fill my mind
with inspiration and creativity
that others may see
the beauty in the world.

Poe

He swallowed death most eagerly
numbness spreading throughout his body
like a fur hide being slowly drawn up.
There wasn't time for remorse or regret -
no, in fact, he welcomed the potential darkness.
It matched the blight on his soul.
Since losing Lenore
(his light, his heart)

he had nothing left but that damnable black bird.
The bottle fell from his weak fingers
shattering on the stone floor
but he barely heard it
over the buzzing in his ears.
It wasn't bad, this dying.
There was no pain, no fear,
just a slow fading,
like butter melting in a warm pan.
Would he see her again?
That would imply an afterlife,
of which he was skeptical.
He would make do with an end to his pain,
escape from unceasing loneliness.
There, that hideous feathered figure
could knock until its beak wore off -
he would no longer answer.
Time became meaningless
as he floated through his last moments,
waiting in this sparsely furnished room
that he would not miss leaving behind.
In his final vision, the candle guttering,
he saw it was still night
and he felt it wryly appropriate
that he would expire before dawn's rays
touched his graying skin.
He slid from this life
unwitnessed,
unmourned,
between one indrawn breath
and the weak exhale,
his passage complete.
Was Lenore waiting there for him,
welcoming him to her bosom
with arms thrown wide?
We may think so, if it soothes us,
and so we shall
for we are more full of life than he,
more vital and sustained.
Quoth the raven,
"Evermore."

Jenny Greenteeth

He left the croft with rod in hand
his luck at fishing for to try.
"Have a care," she said to him,
"Wicked Jenny's been seen nearby."
He paid no heed his mother's words
for Wicked Jen was but a myth,
a tale for bairns to scare them safe,
a story told by kin and kith.

The river winds past farm and field
and gives its fish most readily,
but 'ware ye be whereon it slows
for there that Jenny waits for thee.
Within the reeds she hides in wait
for careless children coming near
and with a splash and flash of teeth
the young ones caught then disappear.

He made the bank in all good time
and soon picked out a likely spot,
set his line and watched the clouds
(but Wicked Jenny he forgot).
For fishing is a waiting game
and patience you must have in spades.
The water noise had lulled him dull
and birds close by sang serenades.

He did not sleep exactly, no,
his mind adrift went here and there
so in his youth and innocence
he daydreamed this without a care.
He felt a tug upon his line -
a fish at last, he thought with glee.
We'll eat tonight, and well indeed,
but lo, it was not meant to be.

He held the rod which bent with weight
and pulled with all his summer might.
So slowly, oh, so slowly came
that fish he dreamt in his delight.
What broke the surface scarred his soul -
wild eyes and teeth of nightmare stuff -
and back he crawled with all great speed.
Alas, his speed was not enough.

She reeked of fish and rotten weeds.
Upon all fours she made the bank
and caught the calf, that meaty log -
into his flesh her green teeth sank.
In agony he wept and screamed
but none nearby did hear his call
and Wicked Jen, she set her task
to rend and bite, to tear and maul.

When evening fell, no boy appeared
triumphant with a fish in hand
and worriedly his mother sat
and slowly came to understand
that ne'er again would he come home -
bad Jen had caught him, swift and sure.
A lonely life ahead of her,
she wept in her discomfiture.

They say that in the river reeds,
that Wicked Jenny lays in wait
for any careless personage,
their bones the depths to populate.
So does it seem conjecture wild?
My tale you may thus disbelieve
but listen to those left behind -
perhaps you'll not have need to grieve.

The Doll

Gepetto examined his newest creation. The wood was smooth
as glass, the paint finely done. Each limb was hale and strong. But
there was something about the eyes that disturbed the old carpenter.
They were just painted, white and blue with a black dot in the
center, the simplest of things. Giving his head a brisk shake, Gepetto
picked up the doll and set it on the shelf at the front of the store, a
good spot for window browsers to see his work. He went about
tidying up, covering the paint jars, setting the brushes in the
turpentine to soak, and moving soiled rags to the bin.
   There was a clatter.
   He turned quickly around to see his new piece had fallen to the
floor. Returning to the shelf, he set the doll up again, checked for
damage (there was none), and made sure it was steady and balanced.
Satisfied, Gepetto left the workroom for his small living space on
the second floor, his thoughts having turned to dinner.

The next morning rose fair, and Gepetto performed his ablutions and made ready for another day of carving. He unlocked the shop door and gave the entrance bell a poke, just to hear the joyful sound it made. He looked around his shop at all the wondrous toys and creatures he had made over the winter months. Business had been slow as of late, but he remained optimistic. Taking down his leather apron, he made his way to his carving bench.

And stopped.

He was quite certain that he had cleaned up well the evening before, but there on the floor were fresh curls and chips of pine. Peering at his bench, none of the tools appeared to be out of place (he was meticulous, as his father had taught him) so he shrugged, figuring he had missed sweeping that area.

By late morning, Gepetto was happily ensconced in another doll, this one about half the size of the previous. There had been a time when he had made such clever tiny toys, but as he aged, he found that his hands and his eyes were no longer able to do such finely detailed work. He missed it, but not being one to despair, he did what creating he could and was content.

A trickle of people had come through the shop – the minister and his wife (yes, he'd love to come by the parsonage for tea, thank you), two young mothers looking for simple toys for their babies (he had just the thing), a man in search of a birthday gift for his niece, and a passel of children who wanted to see what new creations had been made. Not one of them so much as inquired about the doll he had finished yesterday. In fact, no one even looked at it.

As the carpenter closed up for another day, he touched the doll's head and told it reassuringly that someone special would be sure to buy it. Then once again, he climbed the stairs to dinner and sleep.

Waking the next morning, Gepetto donned his good shirt and least patched pants, buffed up his shoes, and walked down the road to the town chapel. He was unsure of what any god or being may have planned for him (if anything), but he loved the music and the sun coming through the stained glass. After the last hymn and the receiving line, he waited outside the building until the minister was done. He followed the good man and his sweet wife into their home where tea and lovely small cookies were served (the wife was an excellent baker). Then Gepetto took his leave and strolled along the side of the river than ran past his town, delighted to hear its laughter again after a long cold season.

Returning to his shop, he paused inside to give his doll a friendly pat and, on a whim, left it a portion of the last cookie he had saved from his tea. Then up and to dinner and bed, as usual.

His dreams were strange that night. He half woke a few times, thinking he could hear noises coming from the shop below, but each time he strained his ears, nothing was evident. He sleepily muttered

something about getting a cat, though he kept a tidy home and mice
weren't too much of an issue, but perhaps they had invaded.

When he next opened his eyes, the sun looked strange. Why, he
had overslept! How very unusual, he thought, quickly dressing and
grabbing some cheese and a hunk of bread. He took his time on the
stairs, though (he knew better than to rush) and crossed the shop
floor to unlock the door.

He smelled it before he saw it.

Turning from the door, Gepetto set his gaze on his workbench.
Yes, the source of the scent was apparent.

Sitting there on the heavy wooden bench was a selection of
very small, very detailed toys of all kinds. Boats and wagons, wee
farm animals, a minuscule table and chair set with (was it really?)
an even smaller set of wooden dishes. Curls of pine littered the floor
beneath.

He stood, stunned, for a time. This was the work he once did,
the intricate carving that had gained him fame. Amazed, he moved
to examine them closer. Who could have done this? His shop door
was locked, he was certain of it. If there was someone in the area
with this kind of talent, surely he would have heard. It was a
mystery with no clear answer.

The bell on the door sang out a merry chime, and a handful of
customers greeted him. Then their eyes alighted on the toys before
him. The folks were instantly charmed, delighted that he was doing
the small work again. As the day wore on, and more customers
came in, every new tiny piece was purchased, as well as a few other
items that had sat on shelving for many weeks. But once again, no
one even looked at the new doll in the front.

When it came time to close up shop, Gepetto, weary but
pleased, set the lock and turned to his new doll. Maybe it's my good
luck charm, thought he, giving a small chuckle. He reached out to
retrieve the cookie he had placed beside the doll the night before,
thinking that a small sweet would be just the thing.

It wasn't there. In fact, not a crumb remained. Well, he thought,
I guess I do have mice. He took a closer look at the doll, and yes,
there were a few chips in it, almost like a mouse's teeth would make.
One on the knee, some on either small wooden hand. Gepetto's brow
furrowed and he looked more closely at the marks. Those hadn't
come from teeth; there were no grooved chew marks, just slim and
fine slices, the kind you get when a chisel or knife blade slips a bit.
Those marks weren't there before – Gepetto was an excellent carver
and was too proud to leave such imperfections.

A movement startled him from his examination. Did... no, it
couldn't be, but he was sure he saw the doll's eyes blink. He stared
at his wooden creation for several moments, wondered briefly about
the vagaries of aging, then sighed and made his way to his living
quarters.

But not for sleep. No, tonight he would wait for those small and subtle noises, and he would either catch a mouse or... or something else.

He waited long, with only a single candle for company. At last, a sound of a wooden block dropped, and perhaps a saw moving across wood. Gepetto crept down the stairs, hiding the candle flame behind his hand, and peered into the shop.

Whittling away, seemingly happily, sat the doll at the carpenter's bench. There were already a number of tiny toys made, and more came swiftly from the doll's wooden hands as Gepetto stood there, amazed and conflicted. Should he make his presence known? Would that destroy this miraculous gift? He didn't want to take advantage of what was surely a magical creature, but it had asked for nothing in return as yet. He appreciated the extra sales and was as delighted as his patrons at the intricacy of the work, (for which he could take no credit).

A small voice spoke in the silence. "He who gave me life, so I offer my blessings in return. The work of his hands begets the work of mine own. Go to your rest, old man, and know that I am content."

Wide-eyed, Gepetto turned and went quietly back up the stairs. He got into his night dress, extinguished the candle, and closed his eyes, sure he would not sleep. But sleep came indeed, and it was restful.

Certain it was all a dream, he skipped his morning meal and trotted (far more quickly than he should) down the stairs. There on his bench was a treasure trove of new creations, brightly painted and delightful, some with moving parts (the wagon really rolled). Not one to shirk, Gepetto got to work carving his share of the wooden toys. Once again, customers flooded in to see the new tiny toys and made many purchases.

At the end of the day, he locked the shop door, kissed the doll's head lightly, and went upstairs.

He had cookies to bake.

Rangoli

Rice powder and colored sands
flower petals and bright stones -
these are the tools
of the art of Rangoli.
Each lace-like design
set before the front door
announces that Lakshmi is welcome there.
A lotus for the love of her

eight petals delicate as dewdrops
set in red, pink, white.
Sacred geometry
forms holy symbols
creating intricate patterns
making the mundane magical.
Trace out the spiral
that brings us within;
spill rice flour for the sparrows
to live in harmony.
Walk to your neighbor's home
and witness the elegance
of their doorway
the message of health
and prosperity.
Come learn the art of impermanence
for as beautiful as Rangoli is
the winds and creatures
will disturb the fine lines
break the design
mix the colors.
What was made, now unmade
shall be made anew
at the next dawning.
There is no sorrow here
only the blessed opportunity
to birth a new pattern
from your center
from your heart
drawing a love note
to the gods.

The Last Full Moon

The last full moon of the year
falls on my birthday
shining its light
on this beak winter eve.
Luscious luminescence
silvers my skin,
shines upon the ice
hanging from my roof edges,
brings out my wild side
sleepless

wandering
called to the woods
to dance with the trees.
Diamonds on the snow,
path across frozen water
leading to another world,
a still and quiet place
beautiful in its starkness -
blacks and grays and shimmering
whiteness.
One breath
of chilled air
drawn in
held
released.
Release.
What needs to be let go?
What should be torn away?
hat, too, held in the palms
of my trembling hands?
I gaze at the memories
that it represents -
exhale,
let it fall
fall away.
The pain shatters,
slips softly to the waiting earth,
vanishes in the winter air,
flows away.
Emptiness,
anticipation and readiness
rather than hunger,
freedom and wisdom
rather than burdens I need not carry.
I turn my face upwards
receiving Lady Luna's blessings
filling with light
clean and pure.
Words of thanks
slip from my lips
rise to the skies
to the waiting ears
of Those who watch over me.

Year's End

How will the days unfold
as the new year
sits upon my doorstep
waiting to be invited in?
Where does my attention
and intention
flow and take the measure
of the quality of my desires?
Everywhere I look
there is magick.
Every endeavor
I set my hand to
is successful.
It has been so
nearly all of my life.
I live happily
in the Hands of the Gods
and my heart sings in gratitude
for their blessings.
Let me qualify
and quantify
as my earth-bound being must,
but let the energies fill me
that I might hear and witness
the most excellent beauty
that this world so freely gives
in every moment.
How will the days unfold?
In every way
and any way,
the sacred Dance,
perhaps unreadable by most mortals,
turning and flowing
day unto night,
night unto day.
To follow in this dance
is a miracle,
an opportunity
for Divine connection.
My soul sings
as I anticipate opening that
midnight door
to let the old pass
gently and with a blessing
and to allow the new

to enter in with silent steps.
It will whisper in my ear,
speak softly in my dreaming,
and show itself in each moment.
I gratefully accept
all the good gifts
the universe has to send me.
So mote it be.

Petroglyphs

Draw on cave walls
lost there forever
leaving your mark
in ochre, in ash.
Art in the darkness
hunters and prey
seen by the fire's
flicker and flash.
Headdress of shaman
head of a stag
schools of great sturgeon
share in the space.
Ten-thousand years
til human eyes see
your history written
on stones in that place.
We can make guesses
of life long ago
of what you endured
in scorch and in snow.
You've left behind pieces
an incomplete story
a marvel, a wonder
that we'll never know.
Men in the grasslands
in packs and in singles
hunted the creatures
that helped you survive.
Women tend children
gathered the grasses
searched out the plant foods
so all would well thrive.
Stories 'round fires

the shadow and show
the prowess of leaders
your grief for the dead.
Tracking the moon phase
from season to season
and facing eclipses
with terror and dread.
When did the first of you
draw on that surface
a half-burned stick stylus
your home's walls the page?
Could you imagine
that after your epoch
your art would inspire
the folk of an age?
We still sit by fires
and draw on the walls
and leave our impressions
that speak to our heart.
Thank you, o ancient ones
ochre and ashes
the tales of a people
rendered in art.

Snow

Awake! For the snow flies
in single crystalline forms
to merge as a whole
upon the slumbering earth.
The low winter sun
shines
and if you soften your gaze
you will see millions of diamonds
sparkling
in each pristine drift.
On the path by the river
between long slender arboreal shadows,
the glisten
of tiny rainbows.
Against a backdrop
of gurgles and splashes,
a miracle
in every shimmer,

beauty
wherever the eye falls.
Who could not be moved
by the many graces
of our Mother?
What heavy heart
would not shake itself free
with a strong pulse
echoing the beat
of Nature?
Find wonder
in simple things
and surely
serenity shall follow.

Fortuna

Lady Fortuna, guide my way,
abundance come to me, I pray.
With the turning of the wheel
bless me sure to hope and heal.
In your golden wake I rise
and I begin to realize
that all my luck does come from you
and blessings many, ills but few.
With your Horn of Plenty, give
the things I need to thrive and live
to best support all those I love
and shine for those who rest above.
Copper coins do I set out
in honor, and I have no doubt
that you accept them with my praise
on each dark night and all fair days.
Let me bathe in waters sweet
and slake my thirst to be replete
so I may sing you songs of joy
with every breath that I employ.
O Fortuna, Lady fair
bless me so that I may share
the goods I may and gifts I bring -
To thee, Fortuna, this I sing.

Ode to a Pack of New Colored Pencils

Where shall we go, you and I?
Which joyful expression
of the rainbow
shall come from your tips
and my hand,
a fingerdance
of discovery?
You're brand new,
sharp like my mind,
full of color
like my imagination,
full of the potential
that lives in my dreams.
Sure, some marks
must be made over,
an imperfect line -
but who is to say,
imperfect
but me?
I'm experiencing
a new way to communicate,
a new flow
the like of which
I have never done.
Inspired by sister
and fellow artists,
I will free my fingers
to go where they may.
It's a nice symmetry,
new journal
and new pencils.
It's an adventure
waiting to begin.

Lorelei Greenwood-Jones

Keys

Keys open the way,
clear the occluded passages
that lead from
desire to fruition,
hope to action,
wishes
to accomplishment.
The right key
opens doors,
invites love in,
shows the way.
They also lock,
keeping you safe,
blocking ills without,
leaving the ravening wolves
to ease their hunger
elsewhere,
barring their pointed teeth
from accessing your
tender throat.
You can keep your keys
on an iron ring,
yours in safekeeping,
to bar or invite
as you will.
With the correct key,
the gates of mystery
swing wide
and a smooth path
of knowledge
is laid out before you
to walk as you choose.
A certain key
can release
what was kept inside,
setting free a flood
of emotion,
lifting high
the caged bird
to sing songs
in your heart.

Love for the Ocean

The ocean brings me peace -
salt sea air
shifting my curls about,
waves whispering
against the sand.
Seagulls cry,
their call a raucous song
of dominance and greed.
Long-legged sandpipers
play tag on the shoreline
running from any
perceived threat
including themselves.
Seashells dot the wet sand
but whether inhabited or not
one never knows
until the truth is sought
within.
My feet
push through the chill water
leaving divots
that are soon filled
and smoothed.
Sweet sea treasures -
a shell, a sand dollar, sea glass -
held in the palm
of my hand,
nature's gifts.
These small things
bring me joy.
I set a finger in the water,
touch it to my lips,
a libation of sisterhood
joining with the salt fluids
of my own body.
Sunlight sparks flare
from tips of oncoming waves,
a diamond brilliance
in fluid motion.
From shore to horizon line
the vast ocean
brings my sight far;
only farther
are the stars.

Lorelei Greenwood-Jones

For the Birds

Birds sing to me
in their own language,
bright tones
and chipper chirps
that I wish I could understand.
Soft and low
do the Mourning Doves call
as the female feeds
on seeds
and the male is nearby
guarding her.
Nuthatches peck
upside down on the feeders
garnering morsels
that other birds can't.
Brave chickadees
whir by my head
peeping their cheerful pips
and high-toned quips
as they pay me no mind
as they find
the seeds I leave.
A lone woodpecker,
the smaller kind,
hangs by clawed feet
and bends for a treat,
his body a curve
arching hungrily.
Dark-eyed juncos
feed below
on what is dropped
as finches fight
for their right
to get a spot
at the hollows
of the seed tube.
A flashy pair
of pigeons
wait nearby
with a cautious eye
to peck
at what's left.
The cedar tree
in front of me
is full

of sound and color
brightening the duller
winter day.
Grateful am I
for birds
and the chirped words
that I can almost understand.

Seeing the Seer

The witch's hut sat in a glade in the forest. A small dwelling, stuffed with character and overflowing with cats, it was cozy in cold weather and just right in warm. The front door had just the right creak – she made sure of it – and the broom that hung over the lintel was more magickal than practical, but she can't be faulted for that. Sometimes you just wanted a bit of bling.

When you step over the threshold, you knew you are welcome. There is always tea and fresh-baked biscuits with honey from her own hives, and sitting at the worn but handsome table, you couldn't help but feel like royalty. That's just the nature of her home, the blessing of her hearth. The tuxedo cat with the kinked tail winds her way around your legs, not imposing but hinting at your desire to give her a pat, for surely such a sweet thing as she deserved no less. Other cats (some you're not sure are corporeal) slink about the kitchen on silent feet.

You converse about general things – daily life, work, how your garden is doing this year. She doesn't pressure you or make hints, but leaves you to find your way to the reason for your visit in your own time. When that time comes, you are comfortable enough to ask of her advice, knowing that while the answer may not be as sweet as the tea, it will be as true and solid as the stones of her hearth. She listens carefully to your query, asking clarifying questions of her own, as any good reader does. She closes her eyes in thought, and you wonder what she sees there. A clock on the mantel ticks softly as though not wanting to disturb her concentration.

At last she opens her eyes and a tender smile lifts the corners of her mouth as she looks at you. Her words are direct and kind. She doesn't speak with riddles or clouds upon her tongue, and you know that the answer she gives you is sensible.

When she is done, she gives you time in which to absorb and consider her wisdom. There is no hurry, no rush to be done here, no awkward silences to fill with chatter or fidgeting. She asks no payment, though you have brought her a small gift nonetheless, and she accepts it with grace. You rise to take your leave and she sends you along with a few biscuits for later. You share parting words at the doorstep and make your way home again, content in the knowledge that your time was well-spent.

The witch's hut sat in the glade in the forest...

Besom Time

Take up your broom
your besom
simple instrument of ash
and birch
and willow;
take it from its place
above the door
where it stands guard
against ill coming within -
shield
safekeeper.
Go to your home's heart
and salt the floor
shaking grains of protection
and purity
to absorb negativity
and pain.
Take up your broom
your besom
and sweep widdershins,
earth-wise,
around the room.
Gather the grains
the detritus of living
the hurts and angry words;
let the salt do its work
to remove all ills.
Sweep sadness out the door
sweep tension away
release anguish.
Take up your broom
your besom
and shake out the remaining cruft
into the out of doors
where the earth, our mother,
will take in and transmute

all unwanted energies
back into the light from whence they came.
And if your broom
your besom
is of a colored metal handle
and plastic bristles,
do not think that the magick
will be any less
for all things come from the earth
and are sacred thereby
though they be made
by the hand of man and machine.
May your heart and home
be cleared of undesirable influences
and may peace prevail.
So mote it be.

Touch

Let the touch of my hand
cool your fevered brow
and the lilt of my singing
lift your heavy heart
for these are the things I can do
to ease your burdens
if I am so allowed.
Let the touch of soft rain
drench your bare skin
and quench the thirst
so deep within you
for water is life.
Let bread touch your tongue
humankind's saving sustenance
that altered our condition
and rescued good people
escaping their oppressors
with flat breads baked on stone.
Let the touch of birdsong
flow into your ears
and find that your soul
echoes each note.
Let the touch of wonder
and awe
buoy you up

as the magick surrounds you
and showers you
with gifts that you so truly deserve.
Let the sunrise touch your eyes
building a fascination of color
tone upon tone
from barely seen to fully blossomed
as day arrives once more
as is promised.
Touch you another being
with the same fears and strengths
passions and imperfections
and know them
in more than name.
Touch you this sacred earth
the soil that gifts you with food
the stones that are of your bones
the trees that shelter you
the smallest of creatures
who deserve your love and respect.
Touch you these open arms
to receive and to give
to hold and to support
to catch and to release
as needs change
and time waltzes by us
with music of its own.
Touch you your own desires
and give them wings
for you are not earthbound
nor are your feet buried
in stone
but merely rooted
in solidity of purpose
that forms a foundation
upon which to build miracles.

Bread

Gather the bowl and light the hearth
and bring the goods, in whole and part,
for baking day begins at dawn
and we shall have our bread anon.

Pour the water, not too hot,
and sugar add to hit the spot
with yeast that blooms for rising, and
the wooden spoon in firm-held hand.

The flour and the salt combine
I pour into this bowl of mine
and stir it well and blend it true
then knead it well when mixing's through.

My hands in dough does bring me peace
and lets the tension held, release.
I push and stretch this lovely dough
then cover with a linen throw.

Now set it in a warmer place
to rise and show it's blossom face
and when the rising's set and done
then open the oven, like a sun.

Delicious scent, oh how sublime,
comes far before the baking time
is done, and teases every nose -
aroma bests out any rose.

Then baking's through, the loaf comes out -
to eat it all would make me stout
but try I will to stop and share
this lovely bread beyond compare.

Lorelei Greenwood-Jones

Mountain

Struggling
to climb that mountain,
no Sisyphus am I
with a boulder burden
impossible to bear.
No, my stones are small
comparatively
and eternity shall not see me
striving still
but resting upon that hill
taking in the view
not gifted to all
not seen by those
who only see the stone ahead of them.
A few of my stones
tumble backward
down the slope -
some I retrieve
but others I release
set free to the whims
of fate.
Choosing what burdens to bear
after the self-imposed weights
I set upon my back
is more freeing than cumbersome
more allowance than restriction.
I no longer will carry
what others should carry.
I will not share in the hindrance
will not set my soul in the syrup
of ill-wrought tears
just for the crumbs of acceptance
that others may toss down
from their high table.
I am richer than they.
There are places
on this upward road
to rest and take stock
to find moments of peace
even delight
and these I shall cherish
as I move ever forward
up that mountain.

Heart's Cry

When my heart
hears your heart cry out
in need or in pain
in loneliness or desire
my heart answers yours
by opening wider.
You'll fit easily inside
with all your burdens and unease
your love and your joy.
Your fears shall cease
as the song of my heartbeat
caresses your soul
and eases your mind.
Lose yourself in our twining rhythms
and cast care away.
You are at the very core
of my being
and the center
of my loving heart.
Ever shall I know you.
Always will I buttress
your flagging spirits
and bruised self-esteem
for you are worthy of love
of caring and support
and in me
those shall always be found.

Thoughts in the Dark

My ears ring in the silence,
a constant susurration
from which escape is sought
though I can go nowhere
for true quiet.
My spirit is uneasy this night.
My fears brought point-sharp
to my attention
harboring ill visions
of an undefined nature

but never wavering
in their piercing of my heart.
Of the things that elude me
I fall into despair;
a broader scope
sometimes brings no relief
but adds further questions
as unanswerable as the previous.
I am a bird calling into a darkness
that is not yet graced by dawn.
Shivering
I take hold of the pale light
shining but dimly
in the space before me
for though there is disquiet
the song is answered
and I take flight.
Of the things that include me
I am brought to joy.
Each day a new story,
each hour a mystery to be unveiled
only when it is upon me
and then it has fled.
I live in a constant now
dappled with illumination from the past
and ambition laced with dreaming
looking to the future
but now, nevertheless
for it surrounds me
encases me
no matter how I struggle else.
Embracing
the possibility of peace
I turn toward the rising sun.

Selkie

My skin, you see,
was taken from me
by a well meaning man
who had a plan
to find a wife
to enter his life
but the skin he stole
has taken its toll.

The sea, it calls
from beyond these walls -
my answer, mute,
by the tread of his boot
to claim his way
by night and day
that I stay near
and live in fear.

Two children born
from my body torn
and they, as I,
swim the sky
for the ocean vast
is curse'd cast -
forbidden, we,
to touch the sea.

This man claims love
from the net he wove -
my love to claim
was e'er his aim
but dark, my heart,
being kept apart
from salted water
whom I am daughter.

I search, I seek
while acting meek
my skin to find,
his skein unwind
let loose the trap
that holds me back
to end his hold,
and leave him cold.

My brothers all
will hear my call
and vengeance bear
when skin I wear
and I once more
hear the ocean roar
and slip within
my Selkie skin.

Lorelei Greenwood-Jones

Thoughts of Love

Partway through loving
there comes a time
to take stock
to reassess
because love is, and should be,
an ever evolving thing.
Stagnation creates apathy
boredom
resentment.
When the shine of dating
has faded from view
and you are left with
the essence of the partner you chose,
ask yourself if you chose wisely.
What lies beneath the faded blossom?
What connected you,
brought you together?
Is there still a living spark?
If so,
it must be tended daily
for love must be fed
as fire is fed
and with air between you
and spaces to grow.
Speak compassionately
one to the other;
touch, hold hands, embrace;
earnest actions and gestures
speak volumes.
The strength of love
heals nearly all wounds
and at times
our tongues are sharp
and can cut, wound.
We get busy
tied up in our lives
and distractions.
But come back to center
to the one who is foremost
in your heart
for there is home
and your comfort.
Love, by its nature,
will bloom and wither
over time,

can change its style
and its presentation
both in giving and taking.
You will love deeply,
sometimes wearily,
yet you will love.
Relationships take work
honest effort,
kind application
and continual effort
to keep the magic alive.
So when you pause,
when you assess,
listen -
listen to what is said aloud
and within the heart
silently.
Search out truth
within and without
though it may not be easy.
Pour energy
back into your dear one's heart
and let them know
that they are cherished
and see the light shining
from their eyes
as the reflection
of their love for you.

Chip

Laughter left her lips,
a sparkling sound
in the cloudy afternoon,
because the chipmunk's antics
were so brisk and quirky.
The wee thing ate her fill
from the tray of seed left for her
and her cheeks were so wide
it was doubtful she would be able
to get back inside the barn
through the so-small crack
in the sideboard.
The chip skittered about,
decided she could not wedge

another sunflower kernel
into her bursting cheek pouches
and made for said crack.
With only a slight wiggle
the chip squooshed her face through,
her body fitting along easily after,
and escaped the porch
for the safety of her nest.
Eyeing the feed tray
the girl fetched more seed
and topped off the low water bowl
specifically left
for such visitors.
She loved the birds
that she fed
who fed her
with birdsong.
A worthy return, she felt.
A movement caught her eye
and the chip ran back
to the seeds.
Before filling her cheeks once more,
the chip looked about,
spied the girl sitting nearby,
and let out a high peep.
Was it a warning?
For it did not seem bothered
by the girl's common appearance.
Was it a chippy thankyou
in gratitude for the good eats?
The girl chose to believe so.
Trust grows over time
just as the chipmunk's trust grew -
it knew there would be food,
knew it would be safe.
It delighted the girl
to provide these things
for a better life for these small creatures
that it might echo out
in ripples through the rest of the world
that all might be fed
and safe.

Carter

When you were but little
we'd snuggle together
on the porch rocker
with a broken seat
blankie over you
just you and your mum.
I let you be adventurous
and afforded you trust
further than your years
because you earned it.
Inventive, imaginative,
you had specific interests
and though it took time
for you to reach a goal
once gained
it was firmly in your grasp
ever after.
As a child
you rarely raised a ruckus
saving it, apparently
for your teen years.
You were angry
and rightly so
having endured difficulties
I wish I could have saved you from.
But our bond
formed early
gained in strength.
In your manhood
you have found yourself
found a life path
so different from previous years.
I've watched you grow
from the difficult teen
into a steady and sensible
young man.
Your work ethic
is astonishingly strong
and I admire that.
You've come into your own power.
You know who you are
and what you want
(and don't want, this is true).
You are a joy to me.
I love you, my son.

The Attack

From a dead sleep
she sensed it -
her prey was nearby.
Slowly she rose
eyes sharp and claws sharper
moved to a spot
where she could see it
her toe points tapping
but inaudible
across the floor.
Slowly
with smooth grace
and grave demeanor
sensing all about her
while singularly focused
on the dim shape beyond.
Aware as any hunter is aware
she circled
circled.
It will not hear her coming.
She will rent and rend
tear and claw
gaining its insides.
She stopped
calculated the leap.
One breath.
Two.
LEAPT!
Yes
the cardboard box was hers.

Ogre

and the ogre said to her
you are unworthy
a liar
selfish
and although she knew
this was not true
he said it
so she believed.

during the third hour
of the next argument
(mostly yelled by him)
she was beaten down
convinced of her failure
vowing to do better
never good enough.

it went on for a year
and a little more
time and again
the hurting
the arguments.

he never physically harmed her
but damage was done
nonetheless.

her friend came over one day
to share her tale of woe
an abusive husband
whom she was leaving.

the more that was spoken
the more she realized
that she was hearing about
her own life
and the relationship
she was enduring
in the so called
name of love.

then she caught the ogre in a lie
heard it spoken
to another in the house
and she began
to plan her escape.

it did not go as planned
but she got away
scars showing
when the balloon popped
at the party
startling her into a corner
hunched in a ball.

the wounds on her soul
took some years to heal
and it was not easy
and she thought a lot
about self-harm.

as the years passed
she began to trust again
to build herself up
to know she was worthy.

no, it was not a smooth road
not in any way
but the stab and spear
of the fear and horror
slid slowly away
until one day
she realized
she no longer feared him
no longer felt the anguish
that he had planted
in the soil of her heart.

she could face him
if they ever met again
she would spit in his eye
and turn her back
leaving him
powerless.

she was free of the ogre.

Dancing Fox

When the fox danced
on his small feet -
russet tail waving
greeting the dawn
as the sun slid slowly
up the trunks of tall trees -
he embodied the joy
of living
sensing all the things
that his exquisite body was able -
the scent of new flowers

the touch of earth on his pads
the taste of cool water
the sounds of baby birds
and the glow
of all living beings around him.
He spoke a sharp yip
and heard his littermates reply
a chorus of siblings
discovering their world.
There were mice to chase
vixens to entice
a place
of endless possibility
and continuing fresh days.
Canny, though not yet wise
the fox found his way
through the forest's depths
down deer trails
and rabbit runs
(and oh! how speedily
did those conies hop)
trotting in his freedom.
Belay the issue of hunting hounds
and sounding horns -
he was alive
and fleet of foot.
The huntsman's guns
were not for him
nor the trap
nor snare.
He evaded them all silkily
and found his way back
to the den of his family
and there to bask
in the warmth of kinship
and share the news
of his adventures.

Rain

Before the rain
he could smell the change
in the air
could sense a kind of pressure
not heavy but enrobing

as though a rich garment
surrounded his body.
He saw the light on the trees
turn pale yellow
as clouds gathered
and the breeze rose.
The scent of petrichor
reached his nostrils
advising him
that rain would soon fall.
He desired the touch
of drops on bare skin
liquid on parched earth
as he was also parched
from living
and feeling.
Willing himself wide open
absorbent
he lifted his arms
lifted his face to the nearing storm.
A drop
another
more
like tiny gems
falling from above
blessing him with the gods' tears.
Water ran down his face
down his chest
pooled in his hair.
Savoring the cool libation
that traced patterns
on his dusty skin
he weighed all the anchors
that kept his soul
from its journey
its destination
weighed them and cast them aside.
He found himself
unencumbered
breathing more deeply
than he had in months.
Rain washed away his fears
because he allowed it.
He welcomed its touch
all those singular drops
moving like dancers
with the sole purpose
of washing him clean.

Why had he ever disliked the rain?
He would never again
walk through rain
with his shoulders hunched
face turned downward.
He would bathe in the gifts
that water brings
clarity
purity
ablution and absolution.
As the rain pooled around his feet
toes swimming in small lakes
he found the flow
the link between body and divinity
and he knew
he would never lose that joy again.

Goddess of Spring

She walked among them
small birds resting in her chestnut locks
full of the grace of springtime
and with as much kindness.
Newborn fawns still nursing
followed in her wake
testing the fresh-sprung blossoms
with curious black noses.
In her passage
trees unfurled bright green leaves
shaken loose by her laughter
from their in-turned selves
welcoming the warm breezes
and the longed-for light.
Lingering snows
melted into the softening earth
and waterways now free of ice
rolled forth in joyous freedom.
And on she walked
gracefully
bringing to life all that seemed dead
wakening those who had slumbered
beneath the cold soil.
Spring had come at last
and it was so welcome.

Lorelei Greenwood-Jones

Thinking About 2020

Wisps of smoke hung in the air
moving steadily in the weak sunlight
coming through the open window.
A pleasant smokey scent, this incense,
evocative of summer nights around the fire,
guitars and voices mingling pleasantly
in the soft seaside breeze.
Missing, though, was the tang of salt air
and the companionship of good friends.
This last year was so different,
vacant and brimming at the same time
with losses sharply felt
but new freedoms finding form as well.
Baffling.
There was enough empty time
to discover that time wasn't the issue
when it came to unread books,
unfinished projects,
chores left undone.
The very meaning of time changed,
became alien and strange
like a funhouse mirror,
misshapen and malformed
but open, too.
Perhaps too open.
Unfilled hours turned determination
to sloth.
Some found themselves,
discovering in the quiet
that voice speaking from within
now that the incessant din had ceased.
Some lost themselves,
set adrift without human contact,
spending far too much time
on screens and in front of televisions.
To only be able to see eyes above masks
created a separation
an alienation -
was that a smile underneath?
A grimace?
Recognition an impossibility
without an entire face,
rendering relationships newformed
to wither and perhaps perish.
Yet others found comfort

and freedom,
realizing that much work
that used to be demanded done
inside a building
could be performed at home.
Time spent commuting
on traffic-laden roadways
was now available.
To still others, disaster,
as public venues
became a hive of infectious possibility
and were shut down,
rendering dry the once-lush ambitions
of those onstage.
The idea of who mattered most
shifted like the desert sands,
burying some, exposing still more.
Recent glimmers of hope,
of delivering a death blow
to the death-bringer,
will alter the course,
but never will life return to what it was.
We see now the division, the inequity,
that we are weathering the same storm
but not at all in the same boat.
Privilege has become an accusation,
survival a desperate need.
Positions have changed, ideas altered.
May it be that we find solutions
in this time of dissolution,
healing of every facet of our lives
from the ailments laid bare,
and a rejoining of humanity
that had become so fragmented.
May it be so.

In the Pond

With an expulsion of air
he broke the surface,
treading while he caught his breath
and his racing heartbeat
slowed toward normal.
His racing thoughts, though,

would require more than breathing.
Looking about, he saw no one
and quickly made for the shore
still half disbelieving
that this forgotten pond
was a gateway,
a watery passage
to the creatures' realm below.
He pulled himself wearily up the bank
and crawled further away -
he knew better than to linger
near the edge,
to dabble a toe in that dark liquid.
Placing his back against a tree
he let out another gust
from his burning lungs.
Air had never been sweeter.
Looking down,
he saw the scratches on his arms,
the tattered remains of his clothing.
He would have to see to those wounds quickly -
gods only knew
what ills may have been hiding
in their claws.
Oh how beautiful they had seemed
at first,
luminescent eyes, pale skin,
tall and slender and regal.
No wonder they lured folk in so easily.
These beings, as though from the depths
of one's finest dreams,
lulled one into complacency
with promises of lush delights
and fantasies fulfilled.
These were not the Fair Folk at all
but their opposite number
though the masquerade
was effective.
His memories came fast -
the pealing bells of their laughter
had made him laugh in return,
but hadn't there been
a tinny edge, a grating sound,
that didn't belong?
He heard it, knew it,
but was ensorcelled all the same.
The loaded feast table,
shining with delicacies both known and unknown,

and he had been fool enough
to have eaten his fill.
Their music, while enthralling,
made a slim tear in your hearing -
somehow the dissonance made sense,
at least at first.
Their entertainments were cruel,
harsh,
but he remained mesmerized
as though viewing finest theatre.
How long had he been there?
Moments? Weeks? Years?
It would remain unknowable
until he sought company
far more human than he had endured.
The whimper he let out
went unheard by him
as he rose unsteadily to his feet,
body still damp with pond water.
One step,
more of a stagger.
Two steps,
putting the horrid pond behind him.
Three steps...
he had to look back.
The wonders that enraptured him
were strong in his mind,
seeping into dark corners,
turning to rot.
Was that music on the cool breeze
that was slowly drying him?
Was that a scent
of stunning comestibles?
He did not know how long he stood,
frozen in fearful wonder,
memories licking at his flesh
like a dog so pleased to see his master.
He began to realize
that his hair had dried almost completely,
that his skin no longer reeked
of the decomposing water weeds.
Dry at last.
There he remained for another few minutes
standing closer to the shoreline
than was comfortable,
yet unable to command his muscles
into motion.
As the very last strand of his hair

gave up the moisture
that had been absorbed,
he felt a change.
He forced his eyes
to gaze down at his feet.
Feet?
They looked terribly dusty
though he was on grass.
Hands?
He fought to lift them -
dusty as well.
Fear flooded through him
but he was immobile.
His neck remained bent,
hands in his sight
as he watched his fingertips
blow away like powder.
The lifting wind took his fingers,
hands,
toes,
feet.
Desiccated, flowing like ash.
The scream that left his lips,
those dry lips,
was rendered inaudible,
passed along that gay breeze
into nothingness.
A pair of hooded eyes
broke the calm of the water -
it knew time
would bring them another.

The Visit

Upon the stone windowsill
she paused,
lighting briefly
to rest from the wind.
He looked up
from within the tower room -

lonely had his days been
and long.
Now he saw her
in her fragile beauty
he not daring to move
lest she take flight.
She bathed in the warmth
radiating out the arched opening
feeling no fear.
He began to speak
soft and low
his words a musical cadence
that caressed her hidden ears
and she turned to look at him.
He smiled, closed-lipped
so as not to show
his carnivorous teeth.
With care
he reached out his hand
and broke a tender portion of bread
from his half eaten loaf
offering it to her.
She cocked her head
intrigued yet not quite daring.
He gently laid the morsel
on the far edge
of the worn tabletop
closest to her
and stepped back.
She let out a small peep
and flew to the offering.
He watched as she pecked
with all seeming enjoyment
and filled her small belly
with the gift.
Another smile shaped his lips
and his eyes softened.
Tipping her head to the side
she looked at the fellow
and appearing to decide
she dipped her head
to her breast
and picked out
a small down feather.
She laid it
beside the remainder
of the proffered meal
chirped once more

and flew out into the night.
A gift for a gift
he thought happily.
Taking up the tiny blessing
he moved to his chair by the fire
and sat
gazing at the middle spaces
a smile on his face
until the dawn rose.

Portside Portents

The sea witch called out the future
in her ragged voice
while those on board shuddered
and curled their bodies inward
against the harshness of her words.
How much must they suffer?
What of this creature's predictions
would come true?
Did their deeds doom them
or was it chance
and she was only warning them
of the future?
Would a starboard sacrifice
ease her anger
casting them a better lot?
Was she angry at all?
These and many more were the thoughts
churning in the minds of the sailors
boiling like poisoned guts
rolling like loose shot
as the ship shifted side to side.
Many crossed themselves
some called out to deities
that they typically profaned.
The captain himself
closed within the great cabin
attempted deafness
via whisky and rum
sought numbness
yet found no peace.
Unable to withstand further torment
he burst out of the door

cutlass in hand
determined to confront this haggard visage
whose screeching portents
scarred the soul
maligned the mind.
He cast his gaze over the stilled water
cursing the lack
of swell and wind
that would move his vessel
from earshot of this harpy.
There he spied her
seaweed in tangled iron hair
bloated and barnacle-covered
pointed teeth giving a further edge
to her barbed words.
"Will ye not cease?" he shouted.
"Will ye not give us ease
and release us from this anguish?"
The sea witch stabbed him with her blazing eyes
and the captain fell back a step.
"Ask ye naught of me, man,
for I shall not deliver," she replied
her voice like a chipped razor
gliding across smooth flesh.
"Ye shall suffer my utterances
til thine eyes run with blood!"
The mighty captain grasped the rail.
"Is there aught I may give you
that this crucification terminate
and I and my men set free?"
She threw her head back
releasing a brittle peal of laughter
that rent his spirit.
"If ye find a man innocent
aboard your ship
then send him to me
and the winds shall return.
But your hopes shall be dashed
for there is no such man
aboard a sailing ship."
The captain stepped back
and turned away, troubled.
There was such aboard, aye
but to purchase their freedom
with an offering like that...
he could not bear the stain
upon his soul.
The unending days of punishment

and distress of his crew
weighed heavily as well.
He faced her again
and the waveless sea.
"What of me, witch?
Innocent I be not
but I am mighty."
She thrust a pointed finger at him
ragged-nailed and pale.
"I seek not might, ignorant man.
I seek one whose innocence
whose untainted life
shall bring me salvation."
The captain turned his face
toward the weather-worn planks
of the deck
his brow furrowed.
"What becomes of him
should I release him to your callous care?"
She bared her gnarled teeth
and he realized she meant it as a smile.
"He shall have new life."
He heard the thump of a bare heel
and turned to find Jasper
the very man of whom he spoke.
"Sir, I shall go to her."
His shoulders were straight
his back unbent.
The captain was in a quandary
as becalmed as his vessel.
"But lad," he spoke hesitantly
"you know not of what she may do."
Jasper gave a small smile.
"That I may ease
this terrible burden
from my brethren and master
fills my heart with strength.
Let me go, sir."
Defeated
the captain let out a hard breath.
"All the gods bless ye, lad."
Jasper moved to the bow
and sent a line of rope over the side.
With a last look and nod
hand over hand he let himself down
to the glassy surface.
He swam to her side
the sea witch

whose castigations had not left him unblemished
but could find no true purchase
in heart or mind.
Staring directly into the captain's eyes
the sea witch grasped Jasper's hand
and raised her other arm aloft
piercing the gray sky.
A blinding spike of light shot down
surrounding the unlikely couple
in a dazzling burst of phosphorescence
and when the captain's eyes cleared
the two were gone.
His belly gripped him with fear
bent him with the loss of not knowing
and the agony of a choice not his.
In the new silence the men from below
began to cautiously come up
from the hold.
They saw their captain
alone in aching grief...

And the wind began to blow.

Moon and Stars

He saw the moon in her eyes
glowing, luminous
hovering in the night sky
above the silver limned trees.
Eyes so pale blue
they were like Arctic ice
wolf eyes
and the moon that adorned them
was the only jewel
worthy of her grace.

She saw the stars in his eyes
twinkling, sparkling
shining in the darkness
like sparks from a campfire
speaking of safety, of comfort.
Eyes so brown
like sweet earth
freshly turned
deep like his skin.

Both reached out a hand
one to the other
longing to close the distance
that separated them.
Their fingertips met
and the air shimmered
his touch warm
hers cool
each complementing the other
each providing
what the other needed.

Their palms met
and they melted into one another
swirling energies
and shared breaths
experiencing sensations and details
that no word could convey.
They sought the light within
adding to the brilliance
that surrounded them.
A silent wind
shifted their essence
sent billows, waves, ripples
across their ethereal bodies
the one form they now shared.

Lost were they
deliciously so
with no beginning and no end
a true melding of spirit
a satisfying harmony
creating a more glorious music
than mortal ears had ever witnessed.
Completely enraptured
unencumbered by gravity
the two-become-one drifted higher
until the night sky enveloped them
absorbed them
their substance now part
of the dreams of humankind
and the gods.

Mist

Smoke on the water
like temple incense
rises above the placid surface
of a long lost lake.
Hidden loons
play find-me in the mist
their eerie calls
echoing
in shimmering whiteness.
Dawn has woken
these early risers
these divers of the deep
with their young behind them
like a string of beads.
The marsh heron
glides silently above
and lands in the shallows
to find his morning repast
his gray plumage
blending like a ghost
among the swirling vapor.
A doe
bends her neck
to sip at the clear water
while her curious fawn
sniffs at the shifting mist
and wonders if it wants to play.
Morning frogs leave the mud
eager for the easy insect
still chilled
from night's cool passing
and begin their cheerful croaking
that is such a part
of summer sounds.
Small fishes dart
just below the surface
like barely-seen images
in a scryer's orb
moving in unison
a dance that echoes
flocks of birds in their flight
turning as one.
The stillness of dawn
slowly breaks
into the myriad sounds

of day
greeted by the beings
that love it best.

Labyrinth

(for Tracy)

Walking the coils
of the seven paths
breathing in deeply
exhaling fully
choosing surrender
opening widely
enter the moment
and let yourself be.
Step by measured step
each placement of foot
a deliberate motion
set without haste
touching earth
connecting
sole to soul.
Release all that's held
all that blocks you
defeats you
hinders forward movement.
Go inward
spiraling in
circling out
as the coils bring you
to center.
There is no hurry
no agenda
no expectations
but purposeful peace.
That last smallest turn
brings you inside
space like a womb
safe, comforting
where you are held
and heard
where you may exult
or weep
meditate

give thanks.
Stay as long as you need.
Hand over heart
hand open to receive
open to the love
love that sees you
that frees you
that accepts you
just the way you are.
As you witness
your beauty
your precious self
know it to be true.
Sip from the cup
offered to you here
brim-full
with sacred sustenance
that satiates
nourishes
heals.
When you're ready
gently take yourself
from this center space
moving once more
around the coils
bringing in
all that blesses you
soothes you.
Follow the golden pathway
that guides you to home
and once you reach
that final hallway
pause a moment
to honor what you were
and what you are
and what you may become.
The labyrinth
has restored you
calmed you.
You have shed
and filled
but not to the top
for a full vessel
cannot receive more.
There is space for you still.

Lorelei Greenwood-Jones

Eaters of the Dead

Squat and gray-green
claws like knives
and shark teeth
come they down
down into the hollows
the shadows
to eat of the dead
the long dead
the newly dead
and all betwixt and between
feeding upon spoiled flesh
and crackling bone
sinew and sucking marrow
dry from the years
or fresh as suckling pig.
Gore-crows dream of such feasting.
Bulging eyes
skinny limbs
but oh
such capacious stomachs.
Noises accompany
this ghastly gastronomy -
the wet schlup
of a foot pried from mud, bootless,
crunching
like hard soles trodding gravel,
grunting
like swine in heat
with similar delight.
Dearly departed
are so much gristle
for creatures such as these,
a mere evening's repast
with not a glimmer of kindness
nor remorse.
Safe in the ground
you thought them,
beyond all harm and care.
It's a good thing
that souls flee the body,
that they discorporate
before standing witness
to such unlovely gluttony.
Loved ones
lain with dignity

now a feast for beasts.
Should you chance
to pass near a graveyard
on any such gory gloaming,
stop up your ears
that you hear nothing
of what transpires below,
for it will change you,
these noises,
whether you set eyes
upon their twisted forms
or only bear the horror
of the sounds
of chewing.

Jade

Between the waves
lies a lawn of jade
crested before and behind
with white foam
as though looking at a gem
set in swan down.
This exquisite tone
mostly seen on gray days
is like a liquid apology
for the dreary skies.
Ocean surface
rough with change
rides with its own rhythm
pulling and cresting
as the tide shifts
from high to ebb
leaving more sand exposed
and leaving seashell castaways
on the tawny shore.
Bands of green
roll in swaths of gray water
bejeweling the calm
after every swell
while loons lunge
piercing the depths
for snacks of small fish.

Lorelei Greenwood-Jones

Persephone

Flower fresh maid
picking blossoms
spies a wonder
in floral form.
Goes she nearer
to gather
and is, herself, plucked
from the field.
Brought to the Underworld
by Hades
whose charms win fair Persephone
and she becomes Queen.
But as young women will
she misses her mother
Demeter
goddess of the earth
and desires to return.
Having consumed
seeds from a pomegranate
she is bound
for half a year
to her duties below.
There is no division for her
no difficult decisions
for she is
both loving daughter
and queen -
we can be also.

Ella

Sitting in the cinders
wishing for a change
a different new direction
her life to rearrange.
Drudgery and ample chores
had become the way -
nothing there would brighten
the tedious day-to-day.
Her sisters to attend a ball,
the Prince who sought to marry
was far too great a burden
for Ella's soul to carry.
As the sisters dressed and preened
Ella stood aside
and tho outward she was composed,
within her heart, she cried.

Off they sped in carriage gay
in haste to gain the palace,
poor Ella was thus left behind
and sorrow turned to malice.
Then *poof* before her stood a sprite
tiny as you please
and held within its hand a wand -
a thought did Ella seize.
"This wand can make your wishes true,"
spoke the little elf.
"There's something you would wish to change?
"Do something for yourself?"
Ella took the proffered stick,
leapt on an aging horse
and rode she to the palace fine
with vengeance her recourse.

She gained the grounds in ample time
and slipped into the hall
past guards and sergeants standing there
and crept toward the ball.
Merry dancers whirled about,
then lo, her sisters spied -
cranky Ella's patience broke,
her dreams no more denied.
She waved the wand toward the girls
so elegantly dressed -
a sudden gasp ran through the crowd

and sisters now distressed.
Their gowns so sparkly now did flow
with piles and piles of mice,
and into pumpkins, slippers changed
that had been oh so nice.

Standing in their petticoats
(the mice had quickly fled)
the sisters, so ashamed, called for
their coachmen, faces red.
Back to home, sobbing low,
ran they to their room
then sought they out the other who
had likely caused their gloom.
To the kitchen, to the place
she was known to flee -
in the cinders, Ella sat,
blameless as could be.
Wide her eyes as she was told
what that night transpired,
claimed she innocence, and so
to bed they all retired.

What's the moral in this tale
of pumpkins, wands, and mice?
To little sisters you should be
so comforting and nice?
Or is it that a person, who
given means to use
power over someone else
might find it hard to choose?
To whom should we assign the blame -
the selfish elder girls?
Or the one who had the wand
with ashes in her curls?
I shall leave it up to you -
this tale is not all done,
but ends for now until I write
an intriguing second one.

Ella, Take 2

There once was a lass named Ella
who dreamed of a princely fella.
Her sisters were mean
and spoiled every scene
and at the poor girl they would yell-a.

Her life was all work and no play,
her chore list grew longer each day.
No matter how well
she did, they would yell,
tormenting poor Ella each way.

Then came invitations – a ball!
How thrilling! But not for them all
for Ella was shunned,
not allowed any fun,
and crying, she fled from the hall.

Soon went Sister One and Sis Two
for finery, dresses and shoes,
and ribbons for hair -
they had not a care
for Ella who suffered the blues.

In fancy ball gowns and a broach
they left in great haste via coach
leaving Ella behind
(they did pay her no mind)
and Ella wished each was a roach.

No sooner the thought in her head
a cuss came from the flowerbed -
a strange little form
so far from the norm -
"Dang roses!" the wee woman said.

Ella stared at her, askance.
"So how would you like a big chance
to get some revenge
on those bitter old hens?
Then put on your Big Girly pants!"

Stunned Ella said, "What do you mean?"
"Your sisters who think they're the queen!
Let's pull a big prank!

Their chains we will yank!"
And Ella, to do this, was keen.

A wand was produced, sparkling bright.
"We'll get you all dressed up tonight!"
In two shopping bags
went Ella's gray rags -
her underdress was quite a sight.

But faster than you can say "crown"
Miss Ella was wearing a gown
of such fancy stuff
and more than enough
complete with a zirconia crown.

"You need to reach palace but quick!
Let's find something fast, something slick."
The woman looked 'round
and spied on the ground
an old and abandoned broomstick.

The woman taught Ella side-saddle
(her poor brain made threats soon to addle)
and up in the air
(not high – did not dare)
"Now git! To the palace! Skedaddle!"

The broomstick zipped over the land
while Ella fought cramps in her hand.
The palace in sight
and coming midnight,
her entrance was certainly grand.

The prince wandered over in style
and the sisters, though it took a while,
screeched, "No! It can't be!
Don't love her! Love me!"
The prince thought them quite juvenile.

He took Ella's hand in a trance
and asked if she wanted to dance.
Each woman there
gave a moan of despair,
jealousy in every glance.

But then the old clock struck its chime.
"I've had such a wonderful time,
but now I must go,

with my sisters in tow."
And onto the broomstick they climb.

The prince called, '"My dear, do come back!
There's nothing you'll want for, nor lack
if you'll be my wife -
such a wonderful life!
Guards! Go ye! Follow their track!"

The three girls made home rightly quick
(and good, cuz Sis One was now sick)
and went to their room,
One and Two deep in gloom,
and El back to ashes so thick.

Then one day, a knock at the door
accompanied by a deep roar
brought all sisters near -
they were startled to hear
the prince knew who he's looking for.

"Dear Ella, would you please be mine?"
Sis One and Sis Two simply whined.
"Why no, sir, you see
you're too fancy for me."
And the prince was aghast she declined.

"But you're beautiful, top head to toes!"
She laughed. "Sir, I'm nobody's rose.
Our dance at your ball
meant nothing at all.
You were foolish to guess and suppose."

"Now my sisters, they aren't very nice
and I wish I could turn them to mice,
but if them you choose
(you have little to lose)
believe me, they will not think twice."

Now two wives, not one, is unique
but before he was able to speak
the sisters screamed, "Yes!
We will change our address!"
And the prince knew he was up a creek.

"But girls," the prince tried hard to say.
"We'll go with you this very day!"
the sisters called out

and then with no doubt
they made sure they were on their way.

So Ella now lives there alone,
her sisters, a castle of stone
and servants to rule
and the prince, no one's fool,
kept firmly upon his gold throne

for Queens One and Two rule the land
and keep poor His Highness in hand
and each whim of theirs,
though it raises his hairs,
is done, as your majesties command.

And Ella, she knows what she wrought,
her freedom so carefully bought
by fooling a prince
with the merest of hints
her sisters a prince they had caught.

Comfort

Where there is pain,
let there be gentleness,
a loving touch
that does not cause wounds to deepen
but soothes and calms,
balm to your aches,
cool water to fever.

Where there is fear,
let there be open arms to enfold you,
a shelter from those
who would do you harm,
a respite from worry,
belief in your story,
compassion.

Where there is dissolution,
let there be connection,
a rebuilding of faith in one another,
coming to terms
and coming to agreement.

Where there is discomfort,
let there be ease,
a space for breathing
deeply and fully,
caring hands to caress you,
solutions tailored to the ills
that beset you.

Where there is confusion,
let there be illumination,
a breakthrough
past which light can shine
and leave no place for doubt to hide,
honest and tender words
that lay to rest
instability and ignorance.

Where there is weakness,
let there be support,
a net to catch you, hold you,
soft place to land,
breaking your fall and buoying your spirit,
answering your needs,
smoothing the carved lines
that mar your fine brow.

Where there is an end,
let there be peace,
for the story goes on,
the path takes a turn
from which you may discover
new and bright venues,
answers futilely sought
turn to clear vision,
refuge found in unlikely places
that bring you home.

In My Power

When I am in my power
little can stop me.
I am beautiful, intelligent,
witty, creative,
caring, kind.
When I am in my power

I can turn my face
from jabs and jibes,
from any who might seek
to take me down.
Straight is my back
and serene my countenance.
When I am in my power
my intent and desires are met
and magick happens.
When I am in my power
I listen to myself
and trust in my own words,
believe my own feelings.
When I am in my power
I seek to lift up those in pain,
to speak for the voiceless,
to bring joy in place of sadness,
and healing where there may be injury.
When I am in my power
beauty surrounds me,
music from the lips of a passerby,
wisps of clouds in the cerulean above.
When I am in my power
I exude love
and pour forth love,
my hand extended,
my heart open,
my soul wide.

For the Love of Music

Silver notes
from harpstrings played
bringing warmth
to an otherwise
chill day.
Golden was her voice
rich and true
each note
joined with harp
rang
touching the depth
of body and bone
to shiver deliciously within.
Cords and strings

vibrating together
whispering tales
of lost love
and found desire
bringing you to
the edge of passion
and leaving you there
wanting.
Melody shifts
bringing release
harmonies lift you
carry you aloft
on a wave of song
setting you down gently
as if to your lover's arms
cradling you
in a sanctuary
of music.

Lorelei Greenwood-Jones

Haikus by Moonlight

blessings of the night
full moon above me, shining
I have found my place

glowing in the dark
changing our seas and oceans
changing our bodies

moving with the tides
flow and ebb and flow again
endlessly turning

great lunar Lady
let me be compassionate
I cannot hold you

closest to our world
reachable just by rocket
flag and footprints lay

how you delight me
faces ever altering
you shine in my soul

I dance beneath you
reflect in my eyes, water
captures your essence

the owl your hunter
the hare your lone companion
and I sit below

shine through my windows
follow me to my dreaming
we shall meet at last

Silliness

We have a yellow duck-press.
It doesn't moosh real duckles
but makes them out of snow -
they're good for many chuckles.
A tiny snow duck army
goes wad'ling o'er the yard.
We might spray them with color
if it's not too hard.
And then there's snowy dragon
with teeth so sharp and long,
but she won't eat the duckies -
instead, they'll keep her strong
by leading all the stray cats
that prowl our neighborhood.
They try to eat my birdies
and that's not very good.
But dragon makes them fearful
with use of fiery breath.
Those cats won't come around again
because they're scared to death.
So ducks and dragon merry
parade our snowy grounds.
And here at Muppington Manor,
silliness abounds.

Lorelei Greenwood-Jones

A Song of Sheep

Sheep gather
on rolling green hillsides
to sample the clover
under warm sun.
Beneath a tree
hat pulled low over his eyes
the sheep-boy
in casual state
tends his mellow charges.
Spring lambs still suckling
romp on the grassy hills -
fluffy white balls
of merriment -
while their mothers
chew endless mouthfuls
of sweet new grass.
The sheep-boy
thoughts drifting idly
toward cheese and mutton
shifts his position
and notes the slant
of the sunlight.
Soon he must lead the flock
back inside the fencing.
Taking up his staff
he whistles sharply
and two dogs come running
to nip at cloven feet
and bushy tails.
Now to the yard
to the grain and water
to the waiting meal
and chores of day's end.
Soon to bed
'neath woolen covers
blow out the candle
and count sheep.

Wondrous Slumber

In the darkness of the night,
sleep comes,
sometimes slipping in
on cloud feet,
softly drawing me
up in its arms.
Other times
it is elusive,
like trying to hold smoke
in my clasped hands,
fading like a sunset -
the colors only stay so long.
The dreams that come
when rest at last
takes me away
are full of marvelous imaginings,
a kaleidoscope,
a visual cacophony.
Pain rarely finds me there.

Perspective

A picture
is a snapshot in time.
It captures the best
and the worst
and all between and within.
Our everyday experiences
are also snapshots,
only the barest glimpse
of someone else's story,
a mere moment
in a lifetime
about which
we know nothing.
The woman at market
yelling at her kids
has three days to find
a new home
with no funding available.
That man

who cut you off in traffic
just got a call
that his wife is on
her deathbed.
You didn't know.
Did you judge
by the fragment
of the picture
that you saw?
We all do.
But for a moment,
perhaps for the next week,
let's look
beyond our assumptions
for there is far more going on
than we can ever know.

Tree

Like a tree
I send out my roots
wide and deep
seeking
connecting.
Breathing through leaves
as my branches
sway in the wind.
Home am I
to small creatures
the owl and the wren
the beetle and the borer.
Squirrels play
among my leaf litter
racing up and down
the length of me
in an endless game
of catch-me.
Deer rest
in my sheltering shadows
ears perked even then
for the sound of danger.
Welcome is the wanderer
the lover of all things growing

to delight in my curves
my towering length
to find the faces
in the pattern
of leaf
and branch
and bark.
Be amazed
that such a mighty being
such as myself
began as a tiny seed
insignificant
forgettable.
Realize that you too
began as seed
and are now
you yourself
significant
memorable
strong.

Shadow Work

The shadows
that separate us
one from another
the rift between
light and dark
need examination
exhumation
not to remove the darkness
and exchange it for light
but to find a way
to live with that shadow
to accept that it is a part of us.
Any movement
between shine and shade
is but a natural rhythm
sometimes controlled by us.
Shadow cannot be eradicated
evicted
only accepted and transmuted
into what we recognize
as better behavior
healthier habits

clearer choices.
This sacred work
shadow work
is rarely easy
nor is it painless
but all change comes from
a place of irritation
a niggling spot within
that will not rest quietly
until we communicate
until we listen.
Bless you, brave one
for entering into this work
for seeking out the harm
the voice that lies.
As you embark
on the greatest journey
of the self
I wish for you
more roses than thorns
but also the understanding
that thorns have their place.
Find that place
and let them decay
let them nourish the soil
of your fertile heart
and bear once more
roses.

On Writing

Once upon a time
t'was an incidental rhyme
that brought her mind to play
with words most ev'ry day.
When she set pen to sheet
(it wasn't always neat)
the words just seemed to flow
inspiration's fiery glow.
Like music were these words
whose lilt had ne'er been heard
before she wrote them down -
they made her laugh or frown
depending on the tone

the fire or cold stone
the light or darkness then
life given from her pen.
Some days the words won't come
the paper, blank and dumb
she growled and cursed bad luck
so vexing to be stuck.
As caught as I am now
a crease does mar my brow
to find the just-right line
or match to coupled rhyme.
With sorrow my back bent
my vestments to be rent
frustration ceases not
I sit here, stuck and caught.
But then a spark, a light
a Muse has come to right
this nagging sense of doom
that dims this sunny room.
Pen to paper on
soon all annoyance gone
as letters, one by one
turn progress into done.
So if the words you ply
seem hidden, seem so shy
then pray your wondrous Muse
will light that inner fuse
that burns within your head
imagination fed
creation brought to be
for you or all to see.

To my Husband

Set among the stars
is my love for you.
We began like starflash
quickly
though not urgently
but with a certainty
of one for the other.
You are my laughter
and my joy;
you are my quiet times

in the healing bosom of nature
sharing in the vision
of beauty all around us.
You are my comfort
during those moments of sadness
those rare moments of madness
arms around me
whispering healing in my hair.
Wondrous imagination do we share
challenging the other
to top the silliness.
Your intelligence and far-seeing
continually astonish me;
the breadth of your knowledge
a fascination.
Grateful am I for your patience
for I am not always at my best
and happily do I echo it
in your times of need.
You are at the very center
of my heart;
your name
the first word on my lips
as I call out blessings.
I cherish you, my beloved.
You are my all.

The Cave

It wasn't frivolity
that caused her
to edge nearer to the hole.
It wasn't only curiosity
(though goodness knew
she had that in spades).
Perhaps the lure
of the Otherworldly
drew her forth,
caused her to release her hold,
to release her fears
and take that final step.
Limestone caves
were common enough in this region,
cliffs and hillsides

littered with crevices
just right for an inquisitive youth
to go exploring.
After all,
hadn't her own brother
shared stories of his own adventures?
Spoken to her of whispered voices,
sparkling lights,
faint music echoing
against stony walls?
Surely this cave
was as likely as any other,
for it was said
that many linked into one system,
like ant runs belowground.
The opening,
tall enough to admit her body,
beckoned
and she complied.
She stayed with the light at first,
letting her eyes adjust
to the gloom.
It was cool in there
and somewhat damp.
Hmph.
Nothing very exciting so far,
she thought,
somewhat disappointed
but also relieved.
If Mamán knew she was here...
no, nine was old enough.
Raising her chin
she took three deliberate steps
into the shaded stone mouth.
Pausing, she listened.
Water dripped musically
somewhere farther in
but that was all.
"Allons," she spoke.
"on... on... on..."
called back her cave voice.
There was a patch of light up ahead
and she moved toward it
listening to the scuff of her steps.
Looking up,
she saw a hole in the cave ceiling.
Dancing dust motes
sparkled in the sunlight,

setting her mind
thinking of fairies
(the storybook kind,
not those as we know them,
as we know better).
Enchanted though she was,
nine doesn't keep its attention long.
She peered deeper...
yes, another dim light.
Her sneakered toes
sent pebbles scattering
as she walked
through the dim tunnel.
Not as bright, this one.
Unease was beginning to set in,
little mouse-feet of disquiet
scurrying up her spine.
The water noise,
intriguing or not,
was still further along,
into the dark.
"Mais non," she decided
and turned back
toward the cave mouth
and the light beam
between she and it.
Yes, back to the dancing dust,
only a few yards to the exit.
Feeling much relieved,
her feet brought her to the opening.
She stepped out.
It was gloomy in here,
damp.
It didn't seem nearly as scary
as her brother had said.
Ah, there,
a bit of light ahead -
no need for fear, was there?
Bravely she walked down the tunnel,
passing shadows,
entering the light
that pierced the dim cave.
Flickers of dust
in the pale beam
made her giggle,
and she blew into the light
setting the specks dancing.
She was feeling a bit tired now,

and a touch peckish.
She turned back to the cave mouth,
took her steps
to regain the entrance
and stepped outside.
The pale light
didn't penetrate far,
but she figured
if her brother could venture
into these wonderful and mysterious places,
then so could she.
There was a patch of light ahead...

Lovenote

Into your jacket
I slipped a love note
quietly
without you knowing
I left my love there
for you to find.
All the little things
without marching bands or fanfare
add up to such a great amount
that it keeps our love alive.
In the next chapter
of the book I was reading
you placed a love note
not knowing when it would be found
but that it would.
Delicious little surprises
tokens of affection
part of the ongoing romance
that is as solid
as it is sweet.
I love thinking
of things you might enjoy
leaving little gifts
sharing adventures.
And when we're old and gray
we'll have wheelchair races
to see how fast
our lips can touch.

Lorelei Greenwood-Jones

Invitation

Go into the glade
the lawn of sweet grasses
with towering trees
that shelter the mosses.
Come into the center
and hear the sweet music
the otherworld whispers
to you as you dance.

Pipes that are playing
and drums that are beating
shall lift the sad heart
and send sorrow fleeting.
Our feet trace the passage
of seasons and starlight -
our eyes offer welcome
a come-hither glance.

Gleaming and gossamer
wings under moonlight
the shadow and shimmer
of bright winking jewels.
The lilting of voices
that sing of the Old Ones
to honor the wonder
without and within.

Dawn once more rises
and brings the soft sunlight
that sends us to slumber
til the next falling night.
Choice you are given
to stay or to wander -
with care and delight
we do welcome you in.

A Warning

Abandon hope,
thou enter here.
Prepare thyself for
strife and fear.
Debris and trash
the path is strewn,
the very timbers
creak with gloom.
What mystery lies
beneath the cloth?
Dare not, do I,
but thou, thou doth?
Then fling it far
and find beneath
the snarling beast
all hair and teeth.
A hell-born stench
pervades the air -
no living thing
can linger there.
And yet yon beast
survives and grows,
but how this is,
no sage'd one knows.
Be cautious, thou,
in this pit of doom -
tis fright'ning, so,
a teen's bedroom.

Lorelei Greenwood-Jones

Of Blessings

Quiet in the house
only broken
by the musical drip
of water into water
and the occasional
gust of wind.
Warm light on golden walls
reminds me of fireglow.
I am sated
satisfied
safe.
This day was blessed
with creativity
a birthing of ideas
and the manifestation
of dreams.
This day was blessed
by friendship
and the support of those
who believe in my work.
This day was blessed
with tender care
of a wound
received without noticing
until he noticed
and stanched the flow.
Quiet in the house
until words of love
floated to me
like wisps of incense smoke
and I am cradled
by that love
against all storm
against any harm.
Blessed.

Lasting Love

When he said he would love her
he meant it.
When she said she would love him
she was unsure

but willing to try.
He wanted forever.
She was hesitant.
She had a history of rash decisions,
peaks and valleys of emotions
untamable in her present state.
He was coming from years of illness,
meeting with death twice,
struggling with the everyday things
that made life possible.
She had dealt with a different illness,
her days no less difficult.
They forged their bond,
spoke the words,
ventured forth into a new way.
No, it wasn't easy,
especially at first.
But they balanced each other out,
the exuberant one
and the quiet one.
Common interests brought them closer,
brought joy to their days.
She learned to be quieter,
he learned to speak more.
They found magic in nature
that they had both grown up loving
and filled their days
with adventure.
As their 10th year passed,
those who had not been able
to be present for their union,
thinking this was another rash decision,
spoke of their gladness
to have been wrong.
She sees them across the ages,
meeting time and again,
and determines to find him
in every new life.
He, too, wants this.
From the wisdom spoken
by one who had, too,
a whirlwind romance of her own,
he and she know, to a positivity,
that they are
indeed
forever.

Lorelei Greenwood-Jones

Minjo and the Lights

Walking down the wooded path
Minjo saw a faint light
in the darkness ahead.
It was quite late;
he really ought not to be
so far from home.
But that light...
blue, flickering...
He could not help himself.
It was so pretty,
like a cold star
moving slowly away
through the slim young trees.
Minjo followed.
Barely heard,
music reached his ears.
What a joyful sound,
he thought,
intriguing,
not like anything
he had ever heard before.
He needed more of it.
Needed it.
On and on bobbed the strange light,
but Minjo kept up,
weaving his way
among aspens and birch,
saplings and stumps.
As Minjo drew nearer,
he began to realize
that the tantalizing glow
was held by...
well, a creature,
a very strange creature
in outlandish clothing
and wild hair.
He started to worry.
You never knew
what odd beings
might be about in the woods
on a night where the clouds
hid the face of the moon.
Then the creature stopped.
Minjo froze,
afraid he would be seen,

caught.
And indeed,
the creature turned its head,
seemed to stare
into the depths of Minjo's wide eyes.
He could take no more,
turned and fled,
beautiful light and tempting music
forgotten.
Brooke looked about.
Had she heard something
scurry off the path
in the forest behind her?
Eh, likely an animal.
She brought her attention back
to the game on her cellphone.

Eagle Watches

Where the mountains rise above the forest
stony in their faces with iron bones
long does the eagle sit and watch
from her rocky perch on high
queen of all she surveys.
Broad-winged, sharp of talon
little eludes her sharp sight.
Taking flight, she circles
(circles drawn on the stones)
stones beneath her hide her prey
(praying they remain undetected)
detecting the smallest of movements
(moving so silently)
silently she strikes.
She returns to the heights
consumes her meal unhurriedly
for nothing will disturb her.
Well-fed, she sets out once more
gliding and soaring in the morning air
not for food but for joy
(joy is deep within the heart)
heart pumping strongly
(strong is her body, her spirit)
spirit of undeniable beauty

(beauty is all around us)
we gaze in wonder.
Those who drew the circles knew her well
understood her patterns
honored the messages she brought.
They danced her ways around the fire
costumes adorned with feathers
(feathers in his hair)
hair unbound and free
(free from earthly weight)
weightless they leapt, dancing
(dancing in the firelight)
fire of life burning deeply within.
Where the mountains rise above the forest
eagle watches.

For the Love of Diversity

What a myriad of things
with which we clothe ourselves -
habits, gestures,
personas,
a stunning array of attire
suited for play acting
and worn for public consumption.
Most of us adorn ourselves
with the things and ways
that society deems ft and proper.
Many seek to blend in,
to be in fashion
but in that, daring little,
straying not far
from the expected.
Fringes
forerunners
freaks -
these are monikers
attached to those
who are not hindered or burdened
by societal dictations
and expectations.
Some make a statement,
others simply seek freedom.
There are enough
cookie cutter personalities

(and lack of personality)
that a certain amount
of frosting and flair
is refreshing.
That which is diversified
is far more healthy
than a homogenous unit.
We are many things
to many people
and another unto ourselves.
The glorious rainbow being
which is yourself
should be celebrated,
acknowledged.
I see you.

Shalott

Was it his betrayal
that truly caused her demise?
That pale maid
floating on the river
boat bumping the shore
as it moved from side to side
in the current -
was there a hint
of accusation on her face?
To be left behind
with only acceptable "women's work" to do
endless bleak days
of weaving and spinning -
her thoughts wove and spun
as her hands
never idle
(for that is the devil's work)
moved of their own volition
in a memory dance
that needed not her attention.
With her limited experiences
her dreams became quickly stale
and she longed for companionship
more than the distant birds
that walked the banks
but never spoke to her.

The same river
the same island
the same walls and window and bedding
(a maiden's bed, no interest there).
Her longing heart
could not communicate
the mysterious sensations
and dreams.
She only knew the ache.
The mirror brought disturbing dreams
that only added
to the unnameable pain.
The emptiness
and silences
wore on her.
Was it any wonder
she took herself to the river's edge?
Sick with unanswered hopes
blighted by shadows
she lay herself down
in that wooden vessel
and surrendered herself
to the whims of water.
Nearing the turreted halls of Camelot
her last breath
left her lips
as she succumbed
to the whispered curse
laid upon her long ago.
And as much as her days
were filled with mystery
so did she leave another
in the trailing wake
of her funereal vessel.

Time

If I could place time
inside a cedar box
kept fresh there
unbothered by wrinkles
or moths
I would keep safe
all my memories of you
our times spent together
both joyful and painful.
I would not hide away
the unhappy moments
because they made us
who we are
to ourselves and to one another.
Precious
these pieces of our lives
valued more than gold
for what metal
can purchase experiences
and what treasure
could ever be costly enough
to replace the us we became?
The power of our shared stories
the wonder of our friendship
tears of sorrow and of laughter -
their worth
defies all riches
wrought by humankind.
And every time
our lives intersect
I shall fill my lungs
with the scent of cedar.

Wolf

With crooked fang and sharp
it rendered the sheep's flesh
giving in
to a powerful hunger
that had more to do with the hunt
than the inevitable kill.
Its muzzle, limned with blood,
was a fearsome thing
crimson below the stark black
of two gleaming eyes.
Grunting and chomping
its keen ears almost missed
the sound of dead leaves rustling
as sly steps
crunched behind it.
It whirled
a fearsome snarl on its wet mouth
ready for defense or offense.
The figure behind stopped
set out its hands
in a supplicating manner.
"Malinda," spoke the figure,
"Ich bin es, Cristof.
Hör auf. Komm nach Hause."
The beast tipped its head
as though trying to make sense
of the words it somehow recognized.
It didn't want to stop
(the warm flesh was a sumptuous feast)
but there was a certain pull
a desire to follow this figure
this Cristof
and it knew that Hause
was a safe place
a warm place.
Its long tongue extended
licking off some of the ichor.
"Kommen Sie."
Cristof turned
not waiting for the beast to follow
but knowing it would.
When he opened the door
to the house
on the edge of the woods

he left it open and unbarred.
Soon enough
the pad-footed creature
face covered in gore
slunk in.
It climbed the stairs
jumped onto the bed
and collapsed in a boneless heap.
Cristof closed the door.
At least it was only a sheep this time
he thought wearily.
When the morning light
touched the panes
it shone golden
upon the stubble-chinned face
of a man
and the bloodied and naked body
of a young woman.
Four weeks of calm
before the next storm
and only time would tell
how bad that weather would be.

A New Story

I shall have to befriend
my inner dialogue
make it amenable
to my changing needs
for I am not a copy of myself
from day to day
but an ever-evolving organism
that shifts and shines in turns.
There are times when I am mighty
and I accomplish great things;
there are times I am small
and afraid
where decisions and actions
are bigger than the world
and set me apart
from my desires.
Like the weather
I change;
like the tides
running to and flowing from

perhaps with a rhythm
but never the same water.
It cannot be asked of me
not even by me
that I remain steady
and same.
Balance is but a fleeting point
and cannot be excepted to remain.
The things I ask of myself
demand of myself
are not always in harmony
with my abilities.
For this have I chided myself
looked upon my own countenance
with derision
accused myself of weakness
and held failure over my head
like a boulder on a string.
What are these words
that I speak to my soul?
Would I ever speak thusly
to a child
a loved one?
Why do I deny myself
my self
the same courtesy
the same tenderness?
My body believes
everything I tell it.
My body believes.
If I cannot love myself
then making friends
with myself
is the first step to healing.
I must take my own heart's hand
hold it gently
softly
and tell it with words so true
that it is
(I am)
worthy
believed
heard
seen
loved.
My body believes
everything I tell it.
I begin my new story now.

Breaking the Shell

Every shell
hides within it
a treasure
whether it be seed
egg
or heart.
Water and warmth
coax the being inside the seed
to break through its encasing walls
and reach for the light.
Once the chick
outgrows its calcium enclosure
it makes a hole
to let the light in
finally emerging
into life
and growth.
When the walls
built around an aching heart
begin to show cracks
love can once again
gain entrance
heal the hurt
repair the damage
that made it harden.
Welcome the treasures
that seek union
with your blossoming heart
for they are stronger
than walls.

Awakening

Sap flows
within wakening trunks
spreading the news
that spring is come.
Birds
that in warmer climes rest
while winter rages

wing their way northward
to summer homes
filling the air
with songs of desire.
The dreams of bears
in their rocky dens
mingle
with rumbles of hunger
from long-empty bellies.
Serpents sleeping
in scaly knots
sense the softening ground
and find their way
to a sun-warmed stone
soaking up spring's goodness.
Brave sprouts
point their faces skyward
eagerly reaching
for the life-giving light.
Stream beds
with their cold isinglass covers
become slowly liberated
begin to murmur
and ice-locked ponds thaw
while deep in the mud
turtles flex their clawed toes
contemplating water weeds
and small fish.
Ermines' fur darkens
transforming
into mink once more.
For that is spring
the transformation
of seeming death
into life.
Growth, birth, and rebirth
in the ongoing rhythm
of the circling planet
that we call home.

Nature's Peace

When I need peace
I go out into the wilds -
the woods, the ocean,
someplace where
there were more trees than people,
more stones than automobiles,
where chickadees or gulls
were the only voices within hearing.

Oceanside,
boulders worn smooth
by the endless tides,
warm in the sun,
are steadying objects,
a grounding force
that hold me
before the rolling sea.
Scotch pines,
their bases littered
with handsome cones,
were each unique
in form and character,
shaped in no small way
by prevailing winds
from the coastal waters.
I can taste the salt air
and it reminds me
that my tears and blood
are of the same salinity.

And in the woods,
where trees spoke
in their own ancient tongues,
I found I could relax
and breathe more fully.
The leaves underfoot
were last year's canopy,
now degrading, dissolving,
becoming dark, rich soil
in which future generations
of trees would grow.
Carpets of moss,
springy underfoot,
were tempting beds
that invited me to lay down

and become small.

For it is during these times
that I know, heart-deep,
I am connected
with the primal Mother force,
the great nurturer and giver
that supports all life.
This love nourishes me
as a babe at the breast
and I feel embraced
by a holy being
far greater than any other.
In her arms
my every fault is forgiven,
my every fear calmed,
and I am held.

Crisis of Faith

There are times that it seems
connection is lost,
that I'm speaking into an endless valley
filled only with scrub and stones.
That sparkling, or serene,
or heart-deep bond I once felt
becomes dim, tight, empty
and I mourn for the feelings
that have fled.
I've found, too,
that "gone" may not mean utterly severed,
not necessarily a complete termination
but a hiatus,
a resting point
from which one can gain perspective,
where one can have
a much-needed rest.
Existing in limbo is never easy.
I yearn for the soul-touch
that set me aflame in earlier years,
to feel the Divine beside me,
surrounding me, enfolding me,

and maybe within me,
to answer that magick
with a resounding Yes!
So quietly,
with a small fire inside me,
I will say yes
and I will wait.

Treasures

Sometimes
the treasures we gather
aren't objects
but memories and experiences,
the view of mountains
surrounding a valley,
the laughter of a rocky stream,
sunlight on the water.
Sure,
I could have picked up
and brought home
that blue jay feather,
that interesting stone,
that gnarled twig
and added them
to my collection.
But somehow, today,
it was more enjoyable
to leave them lie,
to witness them
and feel pleasure
in that moment.
I want to remember
that I can like an item
without having to possess it.
The taste of cool water
was enough;
fresh cool air in my lungs
filled me.
I am wealthy.
My soul is full
of the beauty of the day
and I am at peace.

Lorelei Greenwood-Jones

The Power of Words

All the words
ever spoken to me
are imprinted upon my mind.
Somewhere inside
I remember them all
and they have shaped me
been the cause
of much of who I have become.
All the things
I have thought about myself
have affected me
and how I love myself.
Wounds from sticks and stones
leave no lasting scars
or patterns on my skin
but the slice of a slight
of malice and purposeful cruelty
dig deep
leaving invisible marks.
The healing balm
of a caring heart
allows me to cry out the pain
lets the poison seep
from my spirit
and puddle beneath me
to be absorbed by the earth -
she transmutes the injury
and I am washed clean.
All the words
ever spoken to me
in kindness and love
are also within me.
They have soothed me
calmed me
brought me back to center.
We learn language
from our family's lips
their fears and prejudices
but also their strengths.
We learn the power of "no"
and the power of our first cuss.
But let us also learn the power
of telling someone
that they are seen
heard

believed.
Everyone has a story to tell
and each perspective is unique.
No story can be told
in the same way
by different people.
Every story
falling from every tongue
has rain and rainbows
pleasure and penalty
loss and hope.
No one hearing them
can remain unaffected.
The stories you tell
and that you tell yourself
have power
and they change the listener
as well as the teller.
I want to know your story.
I want to hear your words.
All the words
ever spoken to you
shape you
shape your life.
I want to see your shape.

Blossom to Bone

There's a fire in the head
that opens like a flower
a blossom full of life
that expands and contracts
with the light.
That light is inspiration.
Some appear in full sun
while others are rendered
through darkness
wrought in the dimness
that marks the soul.
Where the light touches
life surges
and reaches upwards
toward its peak

and upon reaching that summit
begins its slow descent
to inevitable closure.
Bones
whether worn inside or out
give structure
strength
form.
Blossoms reveal
enrapture
delight
and in their delicacy
we understand the limitedness
of time.
So there must be both
in any good work
be it art or the body
delight and decay
strength and sweetness.
Each a pivotal part of life
indeed its very essence.
Where we find a new bud
it has come from something else passing.
Where we find finality
there shall we also find new growth
a beginning that heralds
countless generations
before and behind.
From blossom we come
to bone we must
and the time we measure between
is counted
by how we love
not whom or how many
but that we did
in one form or another
love.

May you ever be blessed.

ABOUT THE AUTHOR

Lorelei Greenwood-Jones has been writing since early childhood and her imagination has never failed her. The abundance of nature in her home state of Maine is rich in beauty and inspires much of her writing and daily life.

Lorelei has lived in Maine most of her life. Her interests include writing, reading, camping, crafting, and music. She is also a baker of seriously yummy bread.

To read more about Lorelei and her writings, visit
http://www.lorelei-greenwood.com